A BLAKE HARTE MYSTERY

RIPPLES

ROBERT INNES

A BLAKE HARTE MYSTERY

BOOK 3

OTHER BLAKE HARTE BOOKS

Untouchable
Confessional
Ripples

CHAPTER

ONE

Blake closed the door behind him as he walked into Juniper Cottage, and sighed with relief. His last day, as last days before time off often were, had been busy, irritating, and had a general tone about it that suggested that it was never going to end. But now, he had finally closed the door on his last day before a two week break, and the first thing he was going to do was spend the rest of the evening in front of the television and relax.

Blake pulled his shirt and tie off with force as he ran upstairs to change into the comfiest clothes he owned. He opened his top drawer and was presented with a choice between an old set of jogging bottoms he had owned since long before he had moved to Harmschapel, and a bright blue and green spotty onesie that his best friend, Sally-Ann, had sent him in the post for Christmas. Blake knew full well she had sent it to him as a joke; it was the last thing on earth he would ever be seen by anybody wearing. But, as he pulled it out and rubbed the soft material between his fingers, he had to admit that it did feel and look as though it would perfectly complement an evening vegetating in front of Netflix.

Just as he was pulling it out and debating as to whether he would really consider wearing such a garish item of clothing, there was a knock at the door. He felt thankful for bringing him to his senses. He threw the onesie back in the drawer, pulled a t-shirt on that was hanging over a chair, and ran back down stairs.

"*Darling*!" Jacqueline, his landlady and neighbour from across the road, exclaimed happily as he opened the door. "How are you?"

"Jacqueline," Blake said, already feeling that his evening of relaxation had come to an end. "I'm fine, thanks. What can I do for you?"

With her crimson red hair lacquered thick with hairspray in her usual beehive, Jacqueline pushed past him and into the cottage.

"Am I right in thinking that you now have a bit

of time off from the station?"

"Yes," said Blake cautiously as he closed the door behind her.

"Two weeks off, wasn't it?"

"Yes,"

"Do you have much planned?"

"Well-"

"Because, do I have an offer for you, my darling!" Jacqueline pulled out a leaflet from her coat pocket and waved it in front of him.

"And what would that be?" Blake asked.

She passed him the leaflet and indicated that he should read it. Blake warily took it from her and read aloud.

"*'The Manor of the Lakes, bed and breakfast.'*" He glanced at her. "'Manor of the Lakes?'"

She waved her hand frantically to invite him to carry on reading. Blake sighed before continuing.

"*'Situated near the beautiful Peak District, the manor's grounds lie in a picturesque location where you can truly be at one with nature, no more so than with the manor's critically acclaimed lakes, of which there are no less than two in the gardens alone. When you're not taking in the panoramic views that are merely a stone's throw away from the manor's grounds, we offer a luxurious spa service like no other. Choose from a wide selection of treatments, massages and other such services from our expert staff, before spending the evening dining in our restaurant, located not a five minute walk away from the grounds. Here at the Manor of the Lakes, we guarantee that you will leave feeling like your old self again.'"*

Blake stopped reading and raised a disdainful eyebrow.

"What do you think?" Jacqueline asked smiling excitedly at him.

"It all sounds lovely," Blake replied. "But what does this have to do with me?"

"That's the best bit!" Jacqueline cried. "I know the family, well – I say *know*. An old friend of mine, Polly Urquhart, married into the family a few months ago, just before they opened. She's offered me a fantastic discount – *just* for me. As long as I can persuade three other people to come along."

"Wait a minute," Blake said. "You said you had an offer for me. How much is this going to cost? It doesn't look cheap."

"I told you," Jacqueline said, pulling the leaflet out of his hands and opening it up. "She's offered me a discount. For four people, this would normally cost somewhere in the region of about five hundred pounds – but because it's new and they want to attract as many people as possible, they're doing a week for two hundred!" She held up the inside of the leaflet, waving it around in what she clearly thought was in a tempting manner. "And, with the discount she's giving me, in return for four of us going, we can get a week there for one hundred pounds. Between four of us! Twenty pound Blake, that's all this will set you back! And look at these pictures, don't you think that's worth it?"

"Twenty *five* pound," Blake corrected, taking the leaflet back and examining the contents.

He had to admit, the pictures inside certainly did the place justice. The interior of the mansion boasted sweeping staircases, sparkling chandeliers, and the lakes looked wide and crystal clear.

"A week?" he asked cynically.

"That's right," Jacqueline said, beaming at him. "Come on, Blake. You work *so* hard – you've hardly *stopped* since you came to Harmschapel, most people would be biting my hand off for an opportunity like this."

Blake couldn't deny that life in Harmschapel had been anything but quiet since he had moved to the village. When he had first arrived, he had been thrown straight into one of the most beguiling cases of his policing career, and then, no less than a month ago, he had almost been struck by lightning at the top of the church tower whilst trying, and ultimately failing, to stop a killer from jumping to his death. Despite his reservations, he did feel that he was due a holiday.

"And who exactly did you have in mind to make it up to four?"

"Well," Jacqueline said. "I was thinking we could bring a plus one each. I'm sure I can find *somebody*, and, I was thinking you might want to bring that friend of yours. The pretty one?"

"What pretty one?"

"You know," Jacqueline said coyly. "That nice boy you get along with so well."

"You mean Harrison?" Blake said, his stomach performing a dull somersault at the mention of the name.

"Harrison, that's the one," Jacqueline said, putting her hands together enthusiastically, though Blake suspected that she had known his name all along. "Think of the life that poor boy has had, if anybody deserves a nice relaxing break away from the village, it's him."

It was certainly true that Harrison had not had the easiest of lives. In the relatively short time that Blake had known him, both of Harrison's parents had been sent to prison for the murder of his abusive ex-boyfriend, Daniel. It had also been Harrison's life Blake had been trying to save from the murderer who had jumped from the church roof. As a result, Blake and Harrison had developed a close bond, and it was one that apparently had not gone unnoticed by some of the other villagers, including Jacqueline.

"So," Jacqueline continued, ignoring Blake's attempts to interrupt her. "I'll give my friend a call and tell her to expect us, what – Monday evening?"

"Hang on, *hang on*," Blake said, as Jacqueline started to walk out the door. "Today's Friday."

"I know it is," Jacqueline said, nodding.

"Monday is three days away."

"So?"

"So, what if Harrison can't make it?"

Jacqueline gave him a knowing smile. "You'll think of something. Now, I must dash – I have a phone call to make!" She squealed excitedly, holding the leaflet up in the air and skipped out the door. Blake closed the door with his foot and bit his lip in deep thought. Since the events at the top of the church tower, Blake and Harrison had grown closer, and there was a mutual attraction that both men had openly admitted to. But Harrison, quite reasonably in Blake's mind, had asked for some time alone to come to terms with all the events of the past year, before throwing himself into another relationship.

Blake threw himself on the sofa and exhaled. He did rather like the idea of a week away from the village. It certainly beat any vague plans he had about spending the majority of his time off in The Dog's Tail, the village pub.

Blake was, however, unsure Harrison would take an invitation in the way it was intended. Blake certainly knew what it felt like for love and relationships to be the last thing on his mind. When he had walked in on his own ex-boyfriend, Nathan, in bed with a woman, the last thing he even considered for a number of months afterwards was the possibility of starting again with somebody else. That was until he met Harrison.

There was only one person he could think of to get in touch with. Someone he could always trust to help him think clearly and sensibly. He pulled his mobile out of his pocket and pressed call.

"Hello?"

"Sally-ann." Blake smiled at the sound of her voice.

As usual, whenever he referred to his best friend by her full name over the phone, he could picture her cringing as if he was running fingernails over a blackboard.

"I *was* going to say, '*how are you, I miss you so much,*' but now, you get nothing," Sally said flatly down the phone.

Blake laughed and lay back on the sofa. "I need your advice."

"Don't you always?" The *click* of the kettle being switched on told Blake he had timed his call with her arriving home from the station he had originally worked when he had lived in Sale near Manchester – before he had walked in on Nathan and requested a transfer, as far away from him as possible.

"How was work?" Blake asked.

Sally blew a raspberry at him down the receiver. "Pants. The Superintendent's been at the station all week. You know what Gresham's like around *her*."

Blake rolled his eyes. One of the things he had felt absolutely no qualms about leaving behind when he had moved to Harmschapel, was his old boss, Inspector Gresham. As cold and uptight as he was crabby and unreasonable, his behaviour somehow always managed to intensify whenever he had officers of a higher rank breathing down his neck.

"He had me on my hands and knees scrubbing his floor. Never mind the fact I've got a DUI to interview, and I mean, *waiting* for me to interview him, oh no – it's far more important for the superintendent to be able to see her ugly face in his office floor than it is for me to be keeping scum off the streets." She let out a moan of frustration and then there was a thumping sound from, Blake imagined, her throwing herself down on her sofa. "Anyway," she said. "What can I do you for?"

Blake explained to her about the week away he had just been informed he was going on and the subsequent invitation he was expected to offer to Harrison to join him.

"So?" Sally said, in a tone that suggested she didn't see the problem. "What do you need my advice about?"

"Oh, come on Sally," Blake replied. "You know how things are with me and Harrison. I don't want him to think I'm trying to hurry things along. I've told him he can have as much time as he needs. Christ, if I'd gone through half the things with men that he had, I think I'd turn straight. Failing that, I'd become a monk. The last thing he needs is me putting pressure on him."

"Oh, Blake," Sally chuckled. "You are an idiot sometimes."

"I knew I could rely on you to be helpful."

"Would you like Harrison to join you on this week away?"

"Of course I would," Blake said. "Otherwise it's just me going away with my landlady and some poor sod she pulled the week before. How sad is that?"

"Very," Sally said in a matter-of-fact sort of way. "Who goes away with their landlady?"

"Someone whose best friend is too far away to drag along," Blake said. "You sure I can't persuade you to join me instead? I miss you."

"And I miss you," Sally replied warmly. "And believe you me, if I could, I'd be there waiting for you already. But no chance. Gresham's banned all holidays while the Superintendent's sniffing around."

"I can still come and see you," Blake pointed out. "Judging by the location, it's not that far away from Sale. I'll sneak away one night and we can drink gin."

"Sounds great, but in the meantime, you're going to hang up the phone, go 'round to see Harrison and invite him on this bloody holiday. Look at it as fate, Blake. It sounds *romantic*! Lakes, spas, fine dining, a mansion – do you need there to be cherubs and a string quartet for you to realise the potential here?"

Blake sighed and closed his eyes. "And if he says no?"

"He's not *going* to say no, is he? Honestly, Blake for a man whose job it is to work with the public, you act like you don't have the first clue about how people think. You go in there, and you specify that it's purely a friends set up. You thought he might like some time away from the village – God knows I would if *I* was him. Sell it to him, make him an offer he can't refuse."

"I'll try," Blake said.

"No, you won't try, you'll *do*," Sally said firmly. "Goodbye!"

And with that, she hung up.

Blake laughed heartily and put his phone back in his pocket, stared up at the ceiling, and weighed up his options. Being at home, doing nothing but lying on his sofa wasn't going to get him an answer either way, and Sally was right. If anybody deserved a holiday, it was Harrison Baxter.

Blake stood up and ran upstairs to his room to get changed. Even if Harrison was going to turn down the invitation, there was no need for Blake to look anything other than his best.

Half an hour later, Blake was standing outside of Harrison's cottage, mentally rehearsing what he was going to say. He stood at the door, preparing to knock, but hesitated. Deep down, he felt ridiculous for feeling so nervous. The last time he had felt like this was over six years ago when he had first asked Nathan out on a date, but the seven years age difference he had on Harrison felt like absolutely nothing at all now and any life experience Blake felt he should have accumulated seemed to have deserted him at this particular moment.

"Stop being an idiot," he told himself. *"Hello, Harrison, I was wondering if you'd like to come away for a week, just as friends, no pressure."* Blake took a deep breath and knocked sharply on the door.

After a moment, the door opened and Blake smiled broadly, but his expression quickly changed. "What the *hell* are you doing here?"

Jacqueline beamed happily at him. "Hello, darling. Do come in. Harrison won't be a moment, he's just taken his goat outside to do her business."

She stepped aside to let Blake inside, who walked in, staring at her bemused.

"Don't look so surprised, Blake. If I'm going to go away with Harrison, I thought I at least should get to know him first." Jacqueline sat down, picking up her mug of tea that Harrison had presumably made her, and sipped it innocently.

"You mean you've already asked him?" Blake asked. He wasn't sure if he was annoyed at his landlady for interfering or relieved that he wasn't going to have to ask Harrison himself.

"Of course I have, darling," Jacqueline replied. "I've already rang my friend and booked the mansion.

It's all arranged."

"He said yes?" Blake asked, eyeing the kitchen door in case Harrison walked in before he had prepared himself.

"Well he seemed surprised to see me," Jacqueline said, sipping her tea again. "In fact, I think he was a bit taken aback that I knew where he lived."

"*I'm* surprised to see you and I am also *'a bit taken aback'* that you knew where he lived," Blake returned hotly.

"You know Harmschapel," Jacqueline said. "It's a small village, it didn't take long to ask around. Just a couple of phone calls, really."

Blake leant back and sighed.

"Now, don't be annoyed, darling," Jacqueline said, tapping him on the knee with her hand. "I didn't know whether you'd ask him in time, I needed to get confirmation. I'm not trying to interfere." She shrugged as Blake raised a doubtful eyebrow at her. "Not intentionally, anyway."

Blake shook his head in disbelief. "What did he say?"

"He hasn't really said anything, yet," Jacqueline said. "His goat seemed rather insistent on being taken outside. He looked like he's thinking about it though!"

Blake stood up and ventured slowly towards the kitchen. As he opened the door, he saw Harrison in the garden through the window. His soft features and wavy blonde hair seemed to be complimented by the approaching darker evening light. Betty, Harrison's goat that he had owned since he was a child, was running around his feet, but Harrison didn't seem to be paying her very much attention, instead leaning against one of the wheelie bins, staring into the distance.

Tentatively opening the back door to the garden, Blake stepped outside. Before he could say anything, Betty bleated at him and took a few steps towards him, kicking the ground as if she were a bull about to charge. Blake glared back at her, remembering the last time he had been at Harrison's house and Betty had tried to knock him over. He then looked up at Harrison and smiled.

"Hey."

Harrison jumped slightly, Blake clearly having broken into his thoughts, then stuck his leg out so that Betty couldn't attempt to charge at him. "Blake! Hi, are you alright?"

"I'm well, thanks," Blake said. "You?"

"Yeah, not bad," Harrison replied. "Didn't expect to be entertaining tonight though."

Blake rolled his eyes. "Sorry about Jacqueline. I swear I didn't know she was here.

Harrison nodded. "So," he said, keeping an eye on Betty who seemed to have temporarily lost interest in Blake and was sniffing at a clump of weeds at the back of the yard. "You're going away for a week?"

"Yes," Blake said cautiously. "I didn't know until about an hour ago. She just sort of sprung it on me. Has Jacqueline mentioned where we're going?"

"Yeah, she said about some sort of spa mansion type place? It sounds nice."

Blake leant against the wheelie bin. "Did she mention that we wanted you to come with us?"

Harrison looked at the ground. "Well, she did invite me, yeah."

"I know it's short notice. You're probably working. We just thought you might like some time away, but –"

"I'm not working actually," Harrison said, putting his hands in his pockets. "Jai's given me the week off from the shop. I was owed some holiday."

"You mean you're free?"

Harrison nodded. "Totally. I just didn't know whether *you* wanted me to come or not."

"I do."

"Really?"

"Of course." Blake smiled. "And I know what it must look like – but trust me, I'm thinking purely as friends. Don't think that I'm trying to push anything, it's not like that. No pressure, just some time away from Harmschapel. What do you think?"

"I didn't know whether you knew that I'd be invited or not," Harrison said, looking happy and relieved. "I didn't want you to think that *I* was the one pushing things by just turning up."

"I would never think that," Blake said, glancing down at Betty who had returned to glaring at him from across the yard. "So, you'll come?"

"I'd love to," Harrison said, looking delighted. "I really would."

"Great," Blake said, grinning. "Can you afford it? Jacqueline's got us some deal where it'll only cost twenty five pounds, as well as whatever money you want to bring along. You know what these places are like, they probably charge thousands for a glass of water. I can lend you some if you're struggling?"

Harrison shook his head firmly. "I'm fine for money. The only thing is that I'll have to get somebody to look after Betty. Feed her, let her out, things like that. I'll go ask my neighbour, will you be alright for a few minutes?"

"Yeah, sure," Blake said, pulling his ecig out of his pocket. "I'll keep an eye on her."

"I won't be long."

He walked back into the house, leaving Blake alone with the goat in the yard. She stepped forwards slowly, and bleated loudly at him.

"And you can pack that in," Blake told her sharply. "Otherwise, I'll be making sure he sends you off to a Satanist for the week."

CHAPTER
TWO

The next morning, when Harrison arrived at Juniper Cottage, Blake was already outside, throwing his own suitcase into the back of his car. As Harrison approached him, he looked up and smiled. "Hi there! I was thinking we should maybe stop at a petrol station on the way and get some supplies, "Blake said. "It's going to be quite a long journey, I'm afraid."

"No worries," Harrison said, smiling back. "Been ages since I had a road trip."

"You got everything you need?"

"Yeah, just about I think," Harrison said,

nodding.

Blake turned round to him. "Do you want to put your case in here? There should be room. Doesn't look like you're taking a lot – are you sure it's going to be enough?"

Harrison had wondered that himself and wasn't even sure if sure that what he had brought was suitable. "Yeah, it'll be fine," he lied, hauling his case into the boot of the car.

Blake shrugged as he slammed the car boot down. "I'm pretty sure we'll be near enough to a town should you need anything else."

"I wasn't sure what to bring really," Harrison confessed, nervously putting his hands in his pockets. "I've never been anywhere like this before."

"Don't worry," Blake replied cheerfully. "We'll get you sorted out if we need to." He glanced at his phone and frowned. "I dunno where Jacqueline is. We said twelve."

He wandered across the road to where his landlady lived in the cottage opposite and knocked on the door. Harrison glanced up to the bedroom window and thought he saw a face quickly disappear behind a curtain. He was just about to alert Blake to it when they heard the sound of someone running down stairs. Then Jacqueline opened the door and peered out at them, looking very strange. Her usual tall red beehive was floppy and she did not have a single scrap of makeup on her face.

"Jacqueline?" Blake said, staring at her apparently just as bemused. "Are you ready to go?"

"Oh, darling, I'm not well," Jacqueline replied, her voice extremely croaky. "I've woken up with this terrible flu." As if to illustrate her ailment, Jacqueline coughed loudly. Harrison glanced at Blake. It was not the most convincing cough he had ever heard.

"You seemed alright yesterday," Blake said, his eyes narrowing.

"I know, darling," Jacqueline wheezed back, coughing violently again. "But it's taken all I've got to drag myself out of bed to come to the door. You'll have to just go without me."

"Without you?" Blake exclaimed, raising his eyebrows. "But what about the money? You've paid for our rooms in the mansion, haven't you?"

"Don't worry about that," Jacqueline said, eyeing Harrison through the crack in the door. Harrison could swear she had a slightly mischievous smile on her face. "We can talk about that when you get back. Just go Blake, honestly. The two of you have a lovely time."

"But Jacqueline-"

"Now, I must get back to bed. Doctor's orders!" Jacqueline cried, her voice temporarily returning to normal before she burst into another bout of dramatic coughing. "Goodbye darlings!"

Blake stared at the door as it was slammed in their faces before turning to Harrison, stunned. "I think we might have been set up here."

Harrison scratched the back of his head awkwardly. "Do you still want to go?"

"Yeah," Blake said quickly, before stopping himself. "If *you* want to that is."

Harrison's stomach flipped dully with excitement, but he tried to look casual. "I've got nothing better to do if you haven't?"

Blake glared at Jacqueline's door again, before letting out a reserved sigh and smiling at Harrison. "Looks like it's just you and me then."

Blake had not been exaggerating when he had said that the drive was a long one and it was made ten times longer by the fact that everybody in the surrounding area seemed to be taking advantage of the unusually bright and sunny weather and had set out on exertions themselves. They had to battle with so many traffic jams that by the time they were finally driving through the surrounding villages towards the Manor of the Lakes, the sun had long since set and Blake's headlights were on full power as they both scrutinised the sides of the road for a sign to tell them where to go.

"There!" Harrison exclaimed finally, pointing into the darkness ahead of them. A handwritten sign was sticking out of the road, barely visible until the car's beams illuminated it.

"Thank *God,*" Blake cried. "As much as I'm enjoying this me and you time, it'd be far better sitting in that swanky looking bar in the pamphlet." He glanced across at Harrison. "Are you alright?"

Harrison had rather hoped his nervousness had been kept hidden, but then he remembered that Blake was too good at his job as a detective to be fooled so easily. "I'm okay, I'm just a bit nervous, I guess."

Blake frowned. "About what?"

Harrison sighed and rubbed his eyes, which were now itching with tiredness from the long journey. "Just this, really. I've never done this with a guy before. The whole going away together thing."

Blake gave him a sympathetic smile. "I meant what I said you know. About this just being a mates thing. If that's what you want it to be. There's seriously no pressure. Both of us could do with some R&R and that's exactly what we're going to get. By the look of the pictures, the place is big enough for us not to be in each other's pockets all week if that's what you're worried about."

"No, no," Harrison said hurriedly. "I didn't mean it like that. I do want to spend time with you. I just don't want to mess it up, I guess."

Blake took a long inhalation on his ecig and blew the vapour out of the window. "Would it help if I told you I'm nervous too?"

Harrison could not help but raise his eyebrows in surprise. "You? Nervous? Why?"

Blake laughed. "Oh, Harrison."

"What?"

"For exactly the same reasons you are, blondie. Have you even considered that *I* might be the one that messes things up? I've thought of nothing else since last night."

He took one look at the confused look on Harrison's face and laughed again. "Remember, it's been a long time since I went anywhere like this with another guy, especially one I fancy. Don't hog all the awkward feelings and embarrassment for yourself, trust me."

Harrison could not remember when he had last felt so touched and reassured at the same time. Reaching into the glove compartment, he pulled out the large bag of sweets they had bought from the village shop before they had set off. "Alright. Here's to mutual nervousness then."

Blake grinned as he picked out a toffee from the bag. "Mutual nervousness."

The silhouette of the huge towering manor came into view in the distance. Against the backdrop of the night sky, it look large and imposing. They could just make out the small orange glows of lights through the multitude of windows around the building. "Is that it?" asked Harrison.

"Must be," Blake replied, as he steered the car around the winding roads. "I hope they're still serving food. I'm absolutely starving."

After a couple of minutes of winding roads in which Blake had to stop to allow other vehicles to pass, they finally reached the narrow drive leading directly up the manor.

"First thing I'm doing is walking around for ten minutes," Blake said, sighing with relief. "I've got cramp in places I didn't even know I had."

"You and me both," Harrison agreed, flexing his neck to relieve some of the stiffness. "I don't think I've-"

But then he stopped and stared out of the window. As they began to turn and drive through the large steel gates leading to the manor, the beams of the headlights revealed a figure standing in the darkness. For a moment, Harrison thought it was a statue, but he then realised that it was somebody staring up at the manor in a long dark cloak.

"Who the hell is that?" Blake exclaimed, staring at the figure as they drove past.

Harrison turned around in his seat as they drove away from whoever it was. Through the rear windows, he watched as the figure stepped out into the road and watched them drive away. They couldn't see the stranger's face under the large low-hanging hood attached to the billowing cloak.

"Weird," Blake murmured as they pulled into the car park. "Maybe it's some gypsy woman or something. I've heard the gypsy community is quite common 'round these parts."

"Why were they just standing there staring up at this place though?" Harrison asked as the car finally came to a stop.

Blake closed his eyes in relief as pulled the keys out of the ignition. "I don't know and frankly at this moment, I don't care. How's this for a plan of action? We take the cases in, get our rooms, shower, and change, and then find the bar and have a large glass of a ridiculously overpriced alcoholic beverage?"

Harrison nodded. "Sounds good to me."

They got out of the car and Blake took a brief lap of the small rectangular car park to get his legs feeling normal again before they pulled their bags out of the boot and walked towards the large manor.

The front doors were ornate and looked to be handcrafted. If they had not been in such a rush to get in, Harrison would have taken the time to take in the exquisitely carved designs on the doors but the thought was quickly wiped from his mind when Blake opened the door and the reception area appeared in front of them.

It was the grandest looking room Harrison had ever seen. Hanging from the ceiling was an enormous glass chandelier, with light sparkling through each of the crystals hanging from its frame. The room itself was wallpapered everywhere in white and gold and the floors were layered with thick red carpet. There were doors around them with golden signs on them indicating where the bar, restaurant and downstairs toilet were and just to the side of the huge sweeping staircase was a smaller, but no less grand, reception desk.

Blake strode up to the desk and slammed his hand down on the gold bell that was resting on the side of it. A few moments later, a tall, brown haired and middle aged woman appeared from the office behind the desk and smiled pleasantly at them.

"Good evening, can I help you?"

"Hello there," Blake said. "Sorry we're late, but the traffic has been an absolute nightmare. I was wondering if there was a Polly Urquhart here? I understand she's the one that arranged our booking."

"I'm Polly," she replied. "Was it you I spoke to?"

"No, it would have been a lady called Jacqueline."

"Ah, yes!" Polly exclaimed, smiling broadly. "Spoke to her a few days ago. Very generous of her to give you this little deal of ours. This is for our ears only, but the price difference in what you're paying for this week and what you'd normally pay for a double room is quite astonishing, but we're still a new business so it's worth it to get some new customers."

"I'm sure," Blake began before stopping and staring at Polly. "Sorry, did you say *double* room?"

Harrison's stomach churned slightly. "Jacqueline booked us a double room?"

Blake cleared his throat awkwardly. "We were kind of under the impression we would be in separate rooms." He turned to Harrison and shook his head.

"I'm going to kill Jacqueline. I am actually going to kill her."

Harrison laughed, a little impressed by the way Jacqueline had clearly planned all of this out.

"I see," Polly said, nodding. "I won't ask, would that be easier?" She pulled a pair of glasses on that were resting on a large diary on the desk and slipped them on, before opening the diary up. "Well, as I'm sure you'll be pleased to know, we do of course have two singles if you'd like to change rooms. It's not a problem at all when we're this quiet. We're hoping to get much busier than this of course. But if Jacqueline is anything like she was at school, then her trying to meddle in other people's relationships doesn't particularly shock me. I was very surprised to see her pop up on Facebook, asking about this place. We never even really spoke all that much."

Blake and Harrison looked at each other and laughed in disbelief. "She's ridiculous," Blake said, shaking his head. "But yes, we'll take the two singles please. That okay with you, Harrison?"

"Sounds great to me."

Blake took the keys from Polly and passed Harrison one of them. "Perfect. Two rooms in a gorgeous hotel. What could possibly go wrong?"

"Blake? Is that you?"

Harrison turned to where the Irish accent had come from. Walking out of the bar and staring bemused at Blake was a good looking man with very curly black hair and a rucksack on his shoulder. Harrison was surprised to see Blake looking so horrified.

"What the hell are you doing here?" Blake asked the man quietly.

The man rolled his eyes at Blake and walked forwards. "I'm on holiday, Blake. Why the feck else would I be here?"

"Who is he?" Harrison said to Blake, laughing in bemusement.

Blake exhaled deeply before answering. "This is Nathan. My ex-boyfriend."

CHAPTER
THREE

He looked exactly as Blake remembered him. That same cocksure smile, his curly black ringlets on his head that would have looked stupid on anyone else, his shirt unbuttoned at the top to just about reveal the same amount of curly chest hair. As Nathan raised an eyebrow at Blake, in that same way he always had, Blake felt that he could read his mind and suddenly felt incredibly vulnerable as if Nathan could tell exactly what he was thinking and feeling.

"So," Nathan said, putting a hand casually in his pocket and looking Blake up and down. "How have you been?"

Blake felt incapable of responding. All he could feel was his mind whirring painfully, trying to comprehend why Nathan was standing in front of him. Finally he cleared his head enough to respond. "Fine, you?"

Nathan glanced at Harrison and Blake could instantly tell the assumptions that he was coming to. "Grand, thanks," Nathan said.

There were a few moments of awkward silence. Harrison picked up his suitcase and gestured towards the stairs. "I'll just take my case up. Nice meeting you," he said to Nathan.

Nathan nodded, a cocky grin appearing at the side of his mouth. "Yeah, you too, fella."

Harrison didn't say anything else. He just smiled awkwardly at Blake and then disappeared up the stairs.

"Nice looking guy," Nathan said, indicating towards the stairs. "That your new man, is it?"

"What are you doing here, Nathan?" Blake asked him again.

"I told you," Nathan said. "I'm on holiday."

"Davina here, is she?" Blake replied coldly, the mental image of him walking into his bedroom and finding the two of them in bed together flashing through his mind.

"Yes, she is as it happens," Nathan said, turning his head towards the bar.

"And how's married life?"

"Not bad. We had a nice honeymoon. We went to the Bahamas."

"Lovely," Blake said, attempting not to sound as bitter as he felt. "Well, if you'll excuse me."

"You've got your *man* to get back to," Nathan said, his eyes twinkling in that same mischievous manner that had first attracted Blake to him in the first place. "I'm sure I'll see you around."

"No doubt," Blake said. He picked up his case and walked away, trying to look as unaffected by the encounter as possible. As he started to climb the stairs, his stomach churned and his heart pounded, his skin prickling with an overwhelming sense of anger and bitterness.

Blake walked quickly along the corridor to Harrison's room and knocked on the door. Despite the fact that Blake had a lot of things he felt like saying to Nathan, the majority of them insulting, the last thing he wanted was for Harrison to feel pushed out or uncomfortable.

Harrison opened the door and stood in the doorway. "Hi."

"Look, Harrison," Blake said quickly. "Trust me when I say, I do not know what he's doing here, I don't know why he's here today of all days, but you don't need to worry about anything."

Harrison opened the door wider to let Blake into

the room. "Why would I be worried?"

"Come on Harrison," Blake said, putting his suitcase down and turning to him. "I know what you must be thinking, that this is all going to lead to some big romantic reconciliation with him, but I can assure you that it's not."

"Blake, I don't think that," Harrison said, staring at him in surprise. "I thought I was the paranoid one. I did think you'd probably want to at least say hello to him or something so I left you to it. Are you alright? I know I'd probably be a bit of a mess if I bumped into one of my exes in the middle of nowhere like this – well, both of mine are dead so I'd probably be more than a mess but you get what I mean."

Blake found himself laughing and then shook his head in disbelief. "What the *hell* is he doing here?"

"Have you seen him since you left him?"

"I haven't seen him since I walked in on him in bed with that woman. When I was going 'round to collect my stuff from his house when I was moving to Harmschapel, he always made sure he was out, cowardly arsehole that he is. That was the first time I've seen him. He tried to get in contact when he was getting married but I-" His mind briefly flittered back to when he had gotten drunk, read the invitation, and rang Nathan up in the middle of the night before leaving him a tirade of abuse on his voicemail. "-I ignored him."

"Try not to worry about it," Harrison told him.

He walked across the room to the curtains and pulled them open. "We've got all this to concentrate on for the next week, you'll probably barely see –" He stopped as he looked out the window and frowned.

"What's wrong?" Blake asked him.

"That hooded weirdo. They're out there."

Blake stood up and looked out of the window. The view from where they were, a few floors up, meant they could see one of the lakes that the manor boasted, just past the main gardens outside. Walking slowly around the lake, they could make out the same, eerie looking figure. The wind began to pick up and billowed the cloak around the feet of the stranger and even from the distance they were apart, Blake felt unnerved watching them.

"Stay here," Blake said to Harrison. "I'll go and tell Polly on reception."

"Be careful," Harrison said, not taking his eyes off the figure. "I really don't like the look of whoever that is."

"Don't you worry about me," Blake replied, smiling. "It takes a lot to put the wind up me."

"Just ex-boyfriends, yeah?" Harrison quipped.

Blake laughed sarcastically at him and left the room.

When he arrived at the reception desk, Blake tapped the bell and peered out of the window on the other end of the hall. In the darkness, he could just about make out the glistening of the lake, but from where he was standing he couldn't see anybody walking around it.

"Oh, Blake isn't it?" Polly smiled as she looked out of the office door. "Everything alright in your room?"

"I'm actually here because I was wondering if you were aware that there's some man, or at least I think it's a man, wandering around the grounds?"

Polly's face dropped. "A man? What sort of man?"

"Well, he's got a large hood and-"

"Rupert!" Polly cried suddenly, turning to the open office door. "*Rupert!*"

The office door opened and a tall man appeared, concern etched across his face. He looked to be around Blake's age, but he had a receding hairline and the onset of a bald patch at the top of his head.

"What's wrong?" he asked, staring at the panicked Polly.

"He's out there again," she said, clutching his arm. "The hooded man – Rupert, he's *back!*"

Rupert's eyes narrowed. "Where? How do you know? Did you see him?"

"No, I did," Blake said. "He was outside the main gates when we arrived and I saw him walking round the lake a few minutes ago."

"Right," Rupert said, pushing Polly gently to the side. "Stay here. I'm going to put a stop to this, once and for all."

He strode out from behind the desk and through the large doors.

"Rupert, be careful!" Polly exclaimed as he disappeared.

"I'll go and make sure he's alright," Blake said. "Is this hooded figure likely to do him any harm?"

Polly shrugged, wringing her hands together nervously. "I don't know, I really don't."

Blake nodded and followed Rupert out of the doors and into the grounds.

Once outside, Blake jogged to catch up to Rupert, who was storming towards the lake on the other end of the grounds.

"Rupert," called Blake. "Wait a minute."

"I don't need any guests to get themselves involved," Rupert said sharply, glancing over his shoulder.

"I'm not just a guest," Blake said as he arrived at Rupert's side. "I'm a policeman. A detective sergeant actually. I've dealt with my fair share of intruders, hooded or otherwise."

"This guy isn't exactly your average trespasser," Rupert replied as they approached the lake.

Blake looked around him. The lake's surface was mostly still, with only the slight breeze around them pushing the smallest of ripples across it. Aside from that, the grounds were silent and the hooded figure was nowhere to be seen.

"You're sure you saw him here?" Rupert asked him, looking around. "Which room are you in? It could have been the other lake behind you?"

Blake briefly raised his eyebrows and turned behind him. There was indeed another lake, a little way away from them. It was about the same size and stretched out besides the mansion itself. The only thing between the two lakes was the path they had walked along to get where they were, which led further into the grounds. There was also a small wooden hut, which was positioned centrally to the two bodies of water.

"No, it was definitely this one. I didn't even see the other lake."

"And what was he doing?" Rupert asked him, still looking fervently around.

"Just walking around the lake." Blake shrugged. "Sometimes stopping to look up at the mansion, but that was about it."

"What about earlier? When you arrived?"

Blake wasn't used to being asked this many questions. "Not a lot. Just stood staring at the mansion. I didn't even think he was a real person at first, until he moved."

Rupert sighed heavily and ran his fingers through his hair then started walking back towards the mansion.

"So who is this hooded man?" Blake asked him, having to jog again to catch up to Rupert's long strides. "I take it you've seen a lot of him?"

"You could say that," Rupert said simply. "There's no need for you to concern yourself though. The police we've got round here have never seemed especially interested, so I see no reason why you should be. "Sorry," he said, sighing and turning round to face Blake. "I don't mean to snap. I'm – well, *we* are just under quite a lot of stress at the moment."

Blake nodded. "I understand. This '*hooded man*' been giving you quite a bit of trouble, has he?"

"Oh, I wouldn't even know where to begin," Rupert said quietly, walking back towards the mansion again.

When they arrived back at the front entrance, Polly was waiting outside. "Oh thank God," she said when she saw Rupert. "Are you alright? Did you see him?"

Rupert shook his head. "He'd scarpered by the time we got there." He walked past Polly and back into the reception area. "I need a drink."

"Well?" said a stern voice from behind them.

Blake turned to the reception desk. Standing in the office doorway was a man who looked to be in his early sixties. He had scraps of white hair around the bottom of his scalp and had a pair of silver glasses hanging around his neck on a chain. He was staring at Rupert, his eyes narrowed into slits.

Rupert turned round to him and scratched the

back of his head nervously.

"I'm sorry, Rupert," Polly said quietly. "I had to tell him, he was wondering where you were."

Blake watched the older man walk from around the reception desk and towards Rupert. He couldn't help but feel an intense dislike for him – everything about him seemed to suggest somebody who considered themselves to be above everyone else.

"He wasn't out there, Duncan," Rupert said, appearing to be unable to look the man in the eye.

"Who is that?" Blake asked Polly quietly.

"That's Duncan. Rupert's brother," Polly murmured.

"Of course he wasn't out there," Duncan said, now standing over Rupert and looking down on him with his arms crossed. "Isn't it a funny thing? Both you and your *wife* claim to have seen this '*hooded man*,' this unexplained phantom figure, and yet you never seem to be able to produce any proof, do you?"

"I can't help that, Duncan," Rupert said. "And I swear to you – he *is* real. How else would you explain everything that's been happening here the past few months?"

"I can think of one or two explanations," Duncan said, looking at Rupert as he would something that he had just trod in. "And they're a damn sight more sensible than any of the feeble excuses you've come out with!"

"Oh come on, Duncan," Polly said imploringly.

"Why would we lie about something like this? It's ridiculous!"

"Oh, that's one of the brightest things she's said since you burdened us with her, Rupert!" Duncan laughed, his fake jovial expression instantly being replaced by an intimidating glare as he towered over his brother. "You know, Mother was right about you. Everything she said was just bang on the money."

"Don't even go there, Duncan," Rupert said, attempting to stand up to his full height, which wasn't much compared to the man standing over him.

Duncan merely smirked. "Let's not pretend you could do anything about it. Remember, you have a month. One month for you both to prove to me that this ridiculous spa business is worth destroying my home for." He held his hands out, indicating the reception around him. "So I would suggest you stop trying to make excuses."

He threw one last disgusted look at Polly and stormed away, striding up the staircase. Rupert watched him leave, exhaling slowly to calm himself down.

"Don't let him get to you," Polly said, walking towards her husband and putting her hand on his arm. "You know what he's like. If you rise to him, he wins."

"I will *not* let him treat you like that," Rupert said, his voice shaking. "He has no right."

"We wish you hadn't seen that," Polly said to

Blake. "Sorry. Duncan can be…" she seemed to struggle for the right word.

"A pompous moron?" Blake suggested, smiling warmly. "Don't worry about it. I know my fair share of them. I take it your brother has never actually seen this hooded figure?"

"Not exactly," Rupert said, nodding to his wife that he was feeling alright. "It's a bit of a long story."

At that moment, Blake saw Nathan out of the corner of his eye. He was walking out of the bar, with his arms linked with a woman that Blake vaguely recognised from the night that he had entered his bedroom, unaware of the sight that awaited him in his bed. Davina had dyed her hair since Blake had last seen her. It was now ice blonde, and cascading down her shoulders

"Well," said Blake, watching his ex and his wife climbing the staircase, trying to ignore the angry jealous flip of his stomach. "In that case, mine's a vodka and coke."

CHAPTER
FOUR

Blake smiled at the barmaid as she placed his drink in front of him.

"Thank you, Charlotte," Rupert said, taking his own drink, a neat brandy, from her. "You can close up if you like, I don't think we're going to get many more in here tonight."

"Thank you, Sir." The barmaid smiled as she placed another glass down next to Polly. She picked up an empty bowl from the next table and walked away.

"So," Blake said, taking a sip of his vodka and coke. It tasted smooth, the vodka very distinguishable but not bitter. "Tell me about this hooded figure."

"You're on holiday, Mr Harte," Rupert said. "You don't want to hear about our problems, surely?"

"Trust me," Blake replied. "After the day I've had, I would welcome other people's troubles."

Rupert sighed, then took a long sip of his drink. "I wasn't exaggerating when I said it was a long story. You see, this whole thing started about fifty years ago."

"Fifty?" Blake exclaimed.

Rupert nodded. "Let me give you a brief history lesson. Urquhart Manor is actually a fairly recent addition to the surrounding grounds. I mean you get all of these old country manors that have been passed down generation by generation, but this manor and its grounds were only built in the last century."

Blake took another sip of his drink and leant back in his chair, waiting for Rupert to continue.

"You see, this whole stretch of land actually used to be an old steam railway. You know the sort of thing, fairly short journeys, taking visitors around the outskirts of the Lake District and this particular area used to be the end of the line."

"So?" Blake said.

"The station here used to be owned by the Lomaxs. Now that really was a generational hand down. Right from when there was nothing else on the railways other than steam. Then, as steam began to fall out of use, the line was put up for sale. It had been losing money as more and more people flocked to electric trains and eventually, the Lomaxs couldn't afford to keep running their station anymore." Rupert glanced at Polly, who gave him a reassuring smile and then continued. "The lines were pulled up and my grandfather, Arthur Urquhart, bought these grounds. There's a long history of aristocracy in my family so the money to buy the place wasn't a problem. The Lomaxs' were essentially pushed out. From what I gather, they were originally under the impression that they'd be kept on in some capacity, staff on the grounds or whatever. But my Grandfather decided to just hire his own staff, leaving the Lomaxs' without a penny to their name."

"I don't imagine that went down too well?" Blake asked, pulling his ecig out of his pocket. "Am I allowed to use this in here?"

Rupert waved a dismissive hand in consent, so Blake gently sucked on it as Rupert continued. "No, it didn't go down too well, as you say. It began, what I can only describe, as all out warfare between the Lomaxs and the Urquharts. Frequent vandalism, hate mail, fisticuffs on several occasions should any of my family dared to have ventured into the nearest village where the Lomaxs reside."

"But that was all years ago, wasn't it? What does it have to do with what's been happening round here recently?"

Rupert drained his brandy glass and placed it on

the side of the table. "Just as the manor has been handed down to my generation, or Duncan's anyway, so has the family rivalry. We did think that as the older members of the Lomax family had died, the hatred towards us would die with them. But then, Polly came along."

Blake looked at Polly inquisitively.

"I'm a Lomax," she said, smiling nervously. "Or rather, I *was,* until I married Rupert."

"Ah," Blake said. "I see."

"We like to look at our relationship as a modern day *Romeo and Juliet,*" Rupert said warmly, taking a grip of Polly's hand. "Another drink, Blake?"

Blake nodded. "Please." Rupert took Blake's empty glass and walked across to the bar.

"*Romeo and Juliet,* eh?" Blake chuckled. "Two warring families, with an unaccepted love story in the middle. I can see that."

"As you can imagine, my mum and dad didn't take mine and Rupert's relationship well," Polly said. "Despite the fact that Rupert had absolutely nothing to do with the past hardships my family has had to go through, they just cling on to these resentments that should have been buried long ago."

"Do you talk to your family much?" Blake asked her, blowing his vapour away from them.

"Not really, no." Polly sighed. "They basically disowned me when we announced our engagement. They showed up to the wedding, and I stupidly thought that they had come to give their blessings. All they did was try and disrupt things as much as they could. In the end, we had to call the police to remove them before things got physical."

"Which," Rupert said, returning with Blake's drink, "brings us to the hooded figure."

Blake took a sip from his glass. It was a bit stronger than his first and the vodka sent a warm ripple down his body as he swallowed.

"It first appeared about a week after Polly told her family about our engagement. We were in our room, Polly had just got up to close the curtains when she saw it through the window."

"It was just standing there, in the grounds, staring up at the mansion," Polly added. "We thought at first it was some old gypsy woman or something, so Rupert went downstairs to see whoever it was off."

"By the time I got downstairs, it was gone," Rupert continued. "Then, as the weeks went on, it started appearing more and more. We'd be sat in the bar, or in our rooms and there it would be. Never doing anything, just standing there, clearly trying to unsettle us. We'd ring the police, but by the time they'd arrive, it was long gone. Then one night, I was on my own in the grounds. I had been down to the hut in between the lakes. We sometimes use it as a bit of a private staff room. We have a television in there, sofas, that sort of thing. I'd been watching a film as it happens and when it had finished, I locked up the hut and started walking back towards the mansion. But then I saw it. But it wasn't just standing there this time, it was walking towards me from behind the lakes. I don't know whether it had gotten in through the bushes or climbed over the gate or something. At first, I stood my ground, said that the police were fully aware and that if he or she knew what was good for them, they'd better get lost. I didn't feel anywhere near as brave as I hoped I sounded though. Trying to see who was under that hood was impossible, it was just black. Couldn't see a face at all. And then, they pulled a knife out."

Blake raised his eyebrows in surprise. "A knife?"

Rupert nodded. "And all of a sudden, whoever it was began running towards me, the knife pointing right at me. I had no choice but to make a run for it. It was terrifying, I don't mind telling you."

"I bet!" Blake exclaimed. "Surely you told the police?"

"Of course. I ran back to the mansion, upstairs and straight into our room. Of course, by the time I was at the doors of the manor, I looked behind me and the figure was gone. But yes, I rang the police."

"And?"

"As you can imagine, a family feud of this sort of nature was well known to the police around here," Polly interjected. "We'd called them so much over the previous months in regards to this hooded figure, there's been windows smashed, we had a chicken coop in the grounds that we woke up one morning to find all slaughtered but of course every time they got here, there was nothing for them to see as it had long since scarpered."

"They didn't believe you?" Blake asked, surprised.

"No. Oh, they paid us plenty of lip service. *'Investigations are on-going, we've spoken to the Lomax family,'* that train of thought," Rupert replied, rolling his eyes.

"Has there never been any other witnesses that they could speak to?" Blake asked, bewildered.

"That's the problem," Polly said quietly. "Rupert and I are the only ones who have seen it."

"You're kidding? What, none of the guests, none of the other staff?"

Rupert shook his head. "Nobody. Or at least, nobody has come forward. Not even my delightful brother. He seems to think that we're making excuses because the spa business hasn't been going as well as we hoped, hence why you've managed to get such a cheap discount."

"And yet, he or she was the first thing me and Harrison saw when we arrived?" Blake murmured, sipping his glass thoughtfully. "Why get careless now? I've seen it twice and I've only been here a couple of hours." He sucked on his ecig and blew the vapour out carefully. "Do you think it *is* one of your family?"

Polly sighed. "I don't know. Until that night where Rupert was chased with a knife, I would have said probably. They hate anything to do with the Urquharts, but I don't think they'd ever try to *kill* anyone."

Rupert exhaled. "Something we've learnt to agree to disagree on. Nobody else I know but the Lomaxs have that much hatred towards me or my family. Then, of course on top of this is the fact that our mother is extremely unwell at the moment."

"I'm sorry to hear that," Blake said. "Is she in hospital?"

"No," Polly replied, glancing upwards. "She's upstairs on the top floor of the manor. Cancer. She's in a wheelchair, unable to walk, God love her. All said, it's a pretty full on time for us at the minute."

Rupert downed the rest of the contents of his glass and stood up. "I'm going to bed. Thanks for your help, Mr Harte. I appreciate it. Don't feel you need to make that your last drink, Polly will have to charge you for them though. God forbid Duncan finds out I'm giving out freebies."

"Of course," Blake replied. "Goodnight."

Rupert kissed his wife and walked out of the bar. As Blake watched him leave, he couldn't help but think that Rupert looked like he had the weight of the world on his shoulders. Something about him looked haunted.

"I don't mind handing out one more free drink, if you fancy another," Polly said, tapping him on the knee. "Don't tell anyone though."

Blake was already starting to feel a little lightheaded from the strength of his second drink, but as he finished the contents of his glass, he felt his muscles relax after the long drive and the worry and shock of seeing Nathan began to melt away. He nodded and handed over his glass – he was, after all, on holiday.

"I'll have one too if there's one going," said a voice behind him.

Blake turned to see Harrison standing in the doorway of the bar.

"Certainly," Polly said, smiling warmly. "What'll it be?"

"I'll just have a pint thanks, if that's okay?" Harrison asked, sitting down in the seat vacated by Rupert.

Polly nodded and went to fetch the drinks. There was a few moments silence between the two of them, which Blake filled by sucking on his ecig.

"So," Harrisons said finally. "Did you manage to find that hooded bloke?"

Blake shook his head. "He'd gone by the time we got out there."

Harrison nodded as Polly brought their drinks over.

"I'll just be in the office if you need anything else," she said, giving Blake a knowing look.

Blake smiled awkwardly. "Thanks."

There was a few moments silence.

"How are you feeling?" Harrison asked him at last. "About Nathan, I mean."

"I'm alright I think," Blake replied. "I can't pretend it wasn't a surprise to see him. And not a particularly nice one either. Especially as he's got his wife with him."

"Tell me to mind my own business if you want," Harrison began, before pausing. "Never mind, it's not really anything to do with me."

"Go on," Blake said lightly, sipping his drink. "You can ask me about him if you want."

Harrison looked slightly relieved at Blake reading his mind. "What happened? Like I say, you can tell me to-"

"It's fine, Harrison." Blake grinned. "I mean, come on. It's not like I don't know the ins and outs of *your* past couple of relationships." That was an understatement, considering both of Harrison's past relationships had ended up being scrutinised by Blake in separate police investigations. Blake took a long suck on his ecig. He had mentioned to Harrison in the past about how he had caught Nathan in bed with Davina but had never really elaborated on their relationship before.

"We'd been together for a few years," Blake began. "I met him on a night out." His mind flicked back in time to the strobe lighting and the dry ice machine that had been blowing white smoke around the crowded dance floor. "Something about him stood out. Probably the way he was dancing like an idiot, not caring about the looks he was getting. We started chatting and the next thing I knew we were back at his place. A few weeks later we were an item."

Harrison took a sip of his pint and put it down on the table in front of him. "How long were you together?"

"About five years," Blake replied. "It seemed to be going alright, I honestly thought he was the one, you know."

"Oh, I know," Harrison said grimly. Blake imagined he was remembering his relationship with his abusive ex-partner.

"Exactly. Look, I really don't think you want to hear about my ex," Blake said. "It's not why we're here."

"It's like you said though," Harrison replied insistently. "You know all the ins and outs of my past relationships. And anyway." He cocked his head to the side, with a small smile. "What are friends for?"

Blake chuckled. He couldn't quite decide whether Harrison was feeling insecure or whether he was genuinely interested, but he had to admit it helped being able to discuss the shock of seeing Nathan with somebody.

"So when you found out he was cheating on you, it came out of nowhere?"

Blake took a long suck on his ecig. He remembered the day in question all too clearly. It had been freezing cold and he had been wearing a scarf tightly round his neck, his coat buttoned up right to the top. "I'd finished work early. I'd been going through a stage of not finishing till gone ten, eleven at night, sometimes later, having started from about the crack of dawn. So, that day I thought I'd surprise him. I went to the shop and bought a couple of bottles of wine, thought I'd suggest us going out for dinner, you know the sort of thing."

Harrison nodded but didn't say anything.

"But when I walked in, the first thing I saw was just this trail of clothes leading up the stairs to the bedroom. I mean, he often left his clothes lying around the house, but the last I'd checked he didn't wear a bra or a mini skirt."

Harrison grimaced. "And then you walked into the bedroom and saw what was happening?"

Blake nodded, taking a large swig of his vodka as a familiar sensation of resentment and hurt flooded through him. "He even had the nerve to say it wasn't what it looked like. I mean they were both naked in bed, she was on top of him, but it wasn't what it looked like. The weird thing is that I nearly believed him for a few seconds. There surely had to be a reasonable reason as to why my boyfriend, soon to be fiancé, was writhing around in bed with a woman?"

"What happened then?"

"Once I'd got my brain together, I just turned round and walked out again. I remembered to take the two bottles of wine with me and went straight round to Sally's. And like I said, I've barely been in touch with him since that day."

Harrison leant forward in his chair, holding his pint between his legs. "So there's unfinished business?"

"I wouldn't say that," Blake replied. "But there's things I never said to him. I mean, Nathan – he said a lot of things at the time, but that's what he does. He has the gift of the gab better than any man I've ever met, and that's not necessarily a compliment by the way, but I never really told him how angry I was."

Blake looked down at the floor as he realised that this was the first time Harrison had ever really been the listener since they had known each other. Up to now, Blake had been there, both professionally and as a friend, whenever Harrison's life had been turned upside down, but yet now here they were, with Blake pouring his heart out and Harrison offering support. "I don't think he was ever really aware of how much I had to do in order to get over what had happened. I left my job, my house, and my friends, and just upped and left because I couldn't handle facing him anymore. All that just to try and get over the fact that I didn't have a relationship anymore."

"And did it work?" Harrison asked gently.

Blake cradled his glass, the remaining ice cubes clinking around inside. Three strong vodkas in quick succession were making him slightly more loose tongued that he would have liked, but something at the back of his foggy brain told him there was no point in closing up now. "I thought it had," he said quietly. He glanced up at Harrison, who again didn't respond. He merely sipped his pint and gave Blake a sympathetic smile.

The tiredness of the long day soon began to catch up with them and so, thanking Polly, Blake and Harrison walked up the staircase to their rooms.

"What's the plan tomorrow?" Harrison asked as they reached their corridor. "Do we have to get up early for breakfast?"

"I should think so," Blake said, his eyes feeling heavy. "I'll knock on your door if you like. Don't feel like you have to get up early or anything though."

"Oh, I always do," Harrison replied as they arrived at his door. "The farm nailed that into me - ten is the latest I ever lie in."

Blake nodded. "I'll see you in the morning then."

"Goodnight," Harrison said. "And Blake? I'm really pleased we came here. I'm really looking forward to this week."

"Me too." Blake smiled.

Blake watched Harrison walk into his room and closed his eyes in regret at how open he had been about Nathan. He knew deep down that he didn't just want to be friends with Harrison; his feelings for him were stronger than that. But seeing Nathan again had completely taken the wind out of him. There was so much he had wanted to say to him, so much resentment, so many questions that still needed asking.

Once he was in his room, Blake threw himself down on the bed, and stared up at the ceiling. Despite how tired he felt, Blake lay awake long into the night, his head swimming with confused thoughts that made very little sense to him, and the mystery of the hooded figure wasn't among them.

CHAPTER
FIVE

I n contrast to Blake's restless night, Harrison slept incredibly well. The bed in his room was far more soft and comfortable than his one at home. As soon as he had sunk into the mattress and his head had hit the large fluffy pillows, he had slipped into a deep satisfying sleep, meaning that when he woke the next morning, he felt refreshed and cheerful.

He leant across to the bedside cabinet and checked the time on his phone. It had just gone half past nine and already the smell of bacon and pastries from the restaurant downstairs had wafted its way into the room.

Once Harrison had got dressed, he walked out into the corridor. It looked a bit busier than it had yesterday, with people walking up and down the grand staircase chatting amongst themselves. In the morning light, the mansion looked even more attractive. The sun reflected off the sparkling chandeliers brilliantly and as Harrison walked into the restaurant, the large windows afforded him a panoramic view of the gardens outside.

A young waitress in a white blouse and a black skirt approached him. Harrison smiled cheerfully at her as she pulled out a small notepad and pencil from her pocket. She didn't return the smile, instead merely opening the notepad and scribbling something on it.

"Good morning, can I get you a tea or a coffee?" she asked him flatly.

"Just a tea please," Harrison replied.

The tired looking waitress scribbled his order down on the notepad. Harrison wondered if she was so tired, she was likely to forget the one thing he had asked for.

"Help yourself to the breakfast buffet over there, Sir." She pointed vaguely to the other side of the restaurant with her pencil. "Please let me know if there's anything I can get you."

She snapped her notepad shut and strode off without another word in a manner that suggested that asking her for anything should be very low on Harrison's list of priorities.

Harrison strolled up to the pile of plates that was resting besides the line of heating cabinets where all the breakfast foods were sizzling in dishes. At least, he thought to himself, with Blake not having gotten up yet, he could unashamedly pile his plate without worrying about looking greedy and sure enough, by the time Harrison had reached the end, his plate was piled with a selection of bacon, eggs, sausages, toast, fried bread, and, balancing precariously on top of the bacon, a large chocolate flavoured croissant.

He didn't realise till he was halfway through his enormous breakfast that he was still ravenous from how little he had eaten the day before. As he chewed gratefully on an especially crispy piece of bacon, he considered what Blake had told him about Nathan the night before. It certainly didn't change how Harrison felt about Blake, but he realised that it had felt extremely strange to think of Blake as having a past. Up to now, he had seen him as a tall, dashing and almost immoveable police officer who was far beyond letting silly things like past relationships get to him, but last night Harrison had seen a different side to him. Blake had seemed confused and perhaps even a little bit vulnerable. Blake was one of the most empathic people Harrison had ever met, and it felt almost a little unnerving to see Blake so out of sorts with himself.

Suddenly, the loud slamming of a door reverberated round the restaurant, silencing everyone inside it.

"*Well in that case, you can consider yourself fired!*" yelled a voice from reception.

Harrison craned his neck over to the open door leading out to the reception area. Now everyone in the restaurant had gone so quiet, the arguing voices echoed around even louder.

A woman stormed into view, her blonde hair cascading down her hair. "I would *love* to see you try, Mr Urquhart! What are you going to fire me for exactly? Having an opinion? For having the balls to tell you what a pompous, arrogant, low IQ idiot you actually are?"

She unzipped the dark green gilet she was wearing and threw it furiously in the direction of the reception desk. "You aren't even the one who hired me, you don't have a *say!* But then, you're Duncan Urquhart aren't you? God *forbid* anybody not bow to your every whim!"

At that moment, Polly walked into view, holding her hands out in what Harrison assumed was an attempt to calm the situation.

"*Please,*" Polly said, glancing at the open door to the restaurant and the audience inside it that the argument was being witnessed by. "There's no need for *anybody* to be fired. We can sort this out, if we just sit and discuss this like adults-"

"That woman will work here again over my dead body!" Duncan roared, now stepping into view. Harrison was surprised by how red in the face he had managed to get. The only person Harrison had ever seen manage to get that angry looking was his own father.

The blonde haired woman scoffed and stuck her middle finger up at him and stormed out of the reception. The sound of another, louder door being slammed echoed round the restaurant again, making the diners gasp in shock.

"Let her go!" roared Duncan. "Useless woman anyway."

Polly began to say something but Duncan interrupted her. "And any more from you and you can follow her out the door! As far as I'm concerned, you being married to my sorry excuse of a brother means *nothing.*"

Polly looked down at the floor as Duncan stormed off towards the reception again, and the third loud slamming of a door reverberated through to the restaurant.

Harrison glanced around the restaurant. The guests were murmuring amongst themselves, some looking horrified, others seeming delighted by the entertainment.

Harrison wiped the corner of his mouth with the napkin that was by his plate and walked out to the reception. By the time he got there, Polly was sat on a couch by the front door with her head in her hands.

"Are you alright?" Harrison asked her tentatively as he moved towards her.

Polly looked up at him, her eyes red and puffy. "Oh, yes. I'm absolutely fine."

"Come on, no you're not," Harrison said, sitting down beside her. He pulled out the paper napkin he had briefly used in the restaurant and passed it to her. "Sorry, I just wiped my mouth with that, but it'll be alright for drying your eyes. Promise."

Despite her tears, Polly laughed. "Bless you. That's very kind," she said, dabbing her eyes with the napkin. "I'm very sorry your breakfast was interrupted by that. He hasn't got a professional bone in his body."

"No, it's alright," Harrison said. "Look, I'm told I'm a good listener if you want to talk. I've had some problems myself over the past year, especially with family. I guarantee whatever you've got going on won't shock me."

Polly sniffed and glanced up at the reception desk. "You don't want to hear about my problems, honestly."

"Come on," Harrison said, standing up. "There's a whole garden and two lakes I've not seen in the daylight yet. I'd love a guided tour?"

She looked up at him and smiled. "You're not going to take no for an answer, are you?"

Harrison shook his head.

"Go on then," she said, putting the napkin in her pocket. "And in return, you can tell me about you and Blake. There must be quite the story between you two?"

Harrison sighed. "You could say that, yeah."

"It's honestly gorgeous," Harrison exclaimed, as they wandered round the gardens. "I could get used to living here."

In the light of day, the bright green long stretching lawns and perfectly clipped bushes around the paths leading away from the mansion shone brilliantly in the sunlight and the air was filled with the sweet perfume from the various flowers and fauna that were scattered around. In the centre of the biggest lawn by the car park, there was a large lion head fountain stood, with clear water splashing down its sides in the small pool below. It was a huge contrast to the boring fields around Harmschapel and Harrison's own scruffy backyard area.

"I don't even know if *I* will be for much longer," Polly sighed. "What with Duncan constantly breathing down our necks and the business not going as well as it should be."

"Is money not great?" Harrison asked.

Polly shook her head. "No. Not at all. A week like this, what with the weather being as nice as it is and the offer of a cheap discount, this place should be absolutely jam packed."

"Well, it sometimes takes a while for these sorts of things to get off the ground," Harrison said. "Look at this place, people would be mad to turn down being here."

Polly gave him a small smile. "You'd think. Unfortunately, we haven't got all that much time. As much as it pains me to admit it, Duncan has about as much say in everything as he thinks he does. His mother will be leaving him sole ownership of the manor in her will. And if he doesn't think the spa business is worth losing so much of his property to, he's perfectly within his rights to put a stop to it." She pulled a packet of cigarettes out of her pocket and offered one to Harrison, who shook his head. "Besides," she said bitterly, before lighting the cigarette and inhaling on it deeply. "Even if Duncan had no say, Rupert would still do as he's told. For some reason he looks up to him. He's the only person I know who does."

"He doesn't seem like the nicest of people," Harrison replied.

"He isn't. All the staff hate him. He treats anybody he comes across with complete and utter contempt. The woman you saw arguing with him has worked here for years and just like that, she's gone. Hopefully I can persuade her to stay. Fortunately her husband is staying here for the week, so at least she'll be sticking around."

"What happens if he decides that the spa has to stop?" Harrison asked. "Would you still be able to live here?"

Polly sighed and took a long hit on her cigarette. "I don't know. I really don't. I certainly couldn't live here under those circumstances, but whether that would mean Rupert coming with me, I couldn't say."

As they wandered up the path, they approached the lakes. The morning sun sparkled brilliantly on the water's surface, and the only movement on the larger of the two that Harrison was staring out over was the occasional dragonfly dancing just shy of the surface. "This is the best bit though," Harrison said wistfully. "These lakes are just…" he shook his head, struggling for the right word. "Beautiful."

Polly nodded. "Yeah, I suppose they are. You get used to them after a while. Come into the hut – it should be empty this time of day."

They walked a little further down the path towards the small wooden hut that was situated in the centre of the path between the two lakes. Harrison glanced up at a tall semaphore signal that was sticking out of the ground. "What is-?"

"Oh, I was telling Blake last night," Polly said, pulling a set of keys out of her pocket as they approached the door to the hut. "This whole site used to be a small steam railway. When the Urquharts bought the manor, they decided to leave it there as some sort of historical reminder. All it does is remind me of how my family now hates me and why." She flicked her finished cigarette on the ground and unlocked the door to the hut before pulling the door open and stepping inside.

The interior of the hut was cosy, with a small electric heater in the corner, beneath which was a sofa which just fit between the two walls it was placed between. As Harrison stepped inside, the smell of wood hit his nostrils, reminding him that despite all the efforts to make it look to the contrary, this was just a small wooden hut.

As Polly flicked the light on, she gasped as she spotted someone sat on the end of the sofa, looking miserable. It was the woman who had argued with Duncan in the reception area.

"I didn't expect to see you in here," Polly exclaimed. "Come in, Harrison."

"I'm just getting my things together," the woman said, pushing her ice blonde hair out of her face. "Don't try and convince me, Polly. I'm done. I've had enough."

Polly sighed as she closed the door to the hut behind Harrison. "This is Harrison, he's staying at the hotel this week."

The woman glanced at him as she stormed across the hut to a cupboard that was near the door. "Bully for you."

"I can leave you to it if you like," Harrison said to Polly.

"Oh, don't worry!" the woman said shrilly. "There's nothing more to discuss." She pulled out a rucksack from the cupboard and turned to Polly angrily. "Your brother in law is a bastard and I am not taking his vileness for one more second!"

"Look, come on. There's no need for you to leave-"

The woman slammed the door to the cupboard closed and put the rucksack over her shoulder. "Isn't there?"

"Take the rest of the week off," Polly pleaded. "Then, after that, make up your mind. Your hubby's here, you can have a nice relaxing time, without having to worry about anything. After that, we'll discuss whether leaving is really what you want to do. What do you think?"

The woman sighed. "The last thing I want to do is leave you in the lurch, Polly. But no amount of money in the world is enough to take what everyone here has to take off that man."

"So, give me one last chance to make it right," Polly said, gripping her hand. "Just one. I swear to you, by the end of today we will have reached some form of compromise."

The woman stared back at her resolutely. "After everything that's happened, Polly-"

"I know," Polly replied. "But please. I need you. Me and Rupert need you. Promise me you'll think about it?"

Harrison distracted himself from the conversation by standing by the one window in the corner and looking out to the large glistening lake in front of the hut. Now he was here listening to Polly and her employee having such a private discussion, he almost wished he had stayed at his table and fetched himself some more bacon.

Eventually the blonde haired woman sighed and nodded. "I'll speak to Nathan," she said. "See what he thinks. If he wants to stay, which knowing him he probably will, then we'll talk."

Harrison's ears pricked up at the mention of her husband's name. "Nathan?" he said, frowning and turning round.

The woman nodded. "Sorry, I didn't tell you my name, did I? I'm Davina. You might have seen my husband around, Nathan. Irish bloke. Good looking. A bit too good looking for his own good, if you ask me but we laugh about it."

Harrison took her offered hand and shook it, not entirely sure on how to progress with the conversation now that he realised he was in fact talking to the wife of the man Blake had seemed to be in such turmoil about. "Nice to meet you," he said weakly.

"How's this for an idea?" Polly said, an idea apparently coming to her. "Why don't you and Nathan join me and Rupert for dinner tonight, in here? We'll do the hut up nice, get away from the guests and just have a lovely evening. What do you think?"

Davina smiled. "That sounds lovely, actually. Thank you."

"Harrison, have you got much planned for tonight?" Polly asked, turning to him. "How would you like to come for dinner in here tonight? And of course you can invite-"

"Yes!" Harrison interrupted, trying to talk over Polly using Blake's name in front of Davina but immediately regretting it. "That'd be lovely."

"Great," Polly smiled. "I'll see you both here about seven then?"

Davina nodded. "Great. Thanks Polly. See you later, Harrison. Nice meeting you."

"And you," Harrison said, his smile faltering slightly. "See you tonight."

Polly watched Davina leave the hut and turned back to Harrison. "She's a lovely woman, really. She's had a tough life but then, I suppose, who hasn't? Well, I better get back. Lots to plan for tonight. Thanks so much for your kindness though, Harrison. I'm really looking forward to tonight."

Harrison nodded vaguely. "Me too."

A few minutes later, Harrison walked back into the reception area to see Blake on his way to the restaurant.

"Oh, there you are!" he said, walking towards

Harrison. "God, you weren't kidding when you said you get up early. Already had a walk about the place have you?"

"Yeah," Harrison said slowly. "Look, Blake – I need to tell you something."

"Let me just get something to eat, then you can show me round what you've seen if you like. We should plan what we're going to do today."

"Yeah, about that," Harrison replied quietly. "We've got plans for tonight. And I'm honestly sorry."

Blake frowned. "Sorry? Why?"

CHAPTER
SIX

Blake stood in front of the mirror as he slowly fastened the buttons up on his crimson red shirt, glancing at his phone screen. It was half past six. In half an hour or so, he would be sat in the same room as Nathan and his wife. He would be having dinner, in extremely close proximity, to the man who had cheated on him, and the woman he had done it with.

He tried to make his hair look somewhat presentable, fully aware of the fact that his stomach was performing somersaults. It was an all too familiar sensation and Blake was absolutely furious with himself for feeling it. It was, much to his annoyance, completely impossible to deny that he was nervous. And as he stood, looking back at his reflection, nearly eight years older than the last time he had stood in front of a mirror experiencing these stomach gymnastics, he had to ask himself just who he was trying to make himself look so attractive for. Was it Harrison, the kind hearted, well-meaning guy, not three rooms away from him at this very moment (no doubt performing his ablutions just as frantically), who was the only reason Blake had come to this manor in the first place? Or was it Nathan, the man who Blake had fallen in love with, and who Blake had had such strong feelings for that when it had all gone so wrong, he had felt the need to completely abandon all he knew, just so that he could numb the pain he was feeling? As he irritably flicked his fringe into place, he decided the answer was probably both but he refused to allow himself to consider what the ratio might be.

When Harrison had explained how he had ended up accepting the invite to dinner, Blake had initially been rather annoyed, but he knew that Harrison would never mean to cause him any upset. If Blake considered the matter candidly, getting him and Nathan together in the same room was likely the last thing Harrison would want.

Satisfied that his hair was acceptable for whoever he wanted it be, Blake sprayed some aftershave on his freshly shaved face, then put his phone in his pocket before walking across the room to where his ecig was charging on the desk. As he took a couple of puffs on it, he couldn't help but think about how badly he could do with a real cigarette to take the edge off the nerves.

Blake walked out into the corridor and knocked on Harrison's door. After a few moments, Harrison appeared in the doorway and Blake was taken aback by how good he looked.

Harrison had straightened his blonde hair so that it looked sleek and shiny. He was wearing a smart white shirt that hugged his figure to the point that his muscles, achieved by years of working on his parent's farm, were just visible under the material. The sweet aroma of his own aftershave wafted in the air as he stood in the doorway.

"You look great," Blake told him, enjoying the more welcome flutter in his stomach at the sight of his date for the evening.

"Thanks," Harrison said, giving Blake a small smile. "You don't look so bad yourself. Shall we?"

"We shall, sir." Blake replied, holding his arm out to link with Harrison's. Harrison looked at it for a moment, delighted then closed his room door behind him before linking arms with Blake.

"I know I keep saying it," Harrison said as they walked down the stairs to the front entrance. "But I am sorry about what we're doing. I honestly had no idea who that woman was and I *really* didn't know who her husband was."

Blake sighed. "I know. I'm not going to pretend it's going to be easy watching the two of them play footsie under the table – which he will, by the way. I've known him too long to know he won't try and rub it in my face."

"Do you really think he will?" Harrison asked as the opened the entrance door and stepped out into the cold evening air. "To be honest, I can't imagine you wanting to be with someone as childish as that."

Blake laughed. "You'd be surprised. When I met Nathan, I was going through a stage where I quite liked my men to keep me on my toes. If that meant having to deal with someone who was, shall we say, a tad immature, then that was fine by me. Mind you, catching him in bed with a woman was a tad more than I bargained for. I guess the lesson there is be careful what you wish for."

They walked along the path towards the lakes in silence for a few moments. The night sky was clear and a blanket of twinkling stars looked down on them from above. If he had not been on his way to share a meal with his ex-boyfriend, Blake would have been delighted by how romantic the evening had become.

"Don't take this the wrong way," Harrison said slowly. "But, if it's really bothering you watching him and Davina together, I don't mind if you want to build us up a little bit."

Blake stopped and frowned. "Build us up? What do you mean?"

Harrison looked down at the ground. "Well, you know. If you think he's trying to make himself look better by having a wife and you feel bad about being single."

Blake could not have been more touched by what Harrison was implying, or felt worse about himself because Harrison had felt the need to make such a suggestion.

"Listen to me," Blake said, unlinking his arm and turning to him. "I would *never* use you like that." He took hold of Harrison's hand with both of his own and gripped it tightly. "And for your information, the only time I would ever want to give Nathan the impression that me and you were an item would be if it were actually true. And, after everything you've been through, the last thing I'm going to let you be is a pretend answer to my stupid ex-boyfriend. I care about you too much for that."

Harrison looked up at him, his eyes wide. Blake briefly wondered if he was about to burst into tears.

Instead, Harrison just said, very nervously and quietly, "And I care too much about you for you to be dealing with me after everything that I've been through. I meant what I said when we were sat on that wall Blake. I do really like you."

"I know." Blake smiled, thinking back to when they had been sat on the stone wall on top of the highest hill in Harmschapel, where they had both confessed their feelings for each other. "And I really like you. And I will wait as long as it takes, but we're not starting a relationship with you playing a role. Alright? But thank you. I really mean that."

Harrison didn't break his gaze into Blake eyes. For a few moments, neither of them moved. Blake studied Harrison carefully, debating whether the moment was right to lean in towards him for a kiss. But then, before he could even move his head an inch forwards, a familiar voice rang out behind them.

"Aw, isn't that romantic?"

Blake's face dropped as he realised that Nathan was walking towards them. "We're going to put a pin in this moment, alright?" he said to Harrison, who just laughed softly and nodded.

Blake looked down the path to where his ex-boyfriend was striding towards them. "Now Blake, don't let me stop you," Nathan said, the Irish twang in his voice as strong as ever.

"And yet, here we are," Blake replied sarcastically.

Nathan rolled his eyes as he arrived at Blake's side. "Still as hilarious as ever. Davina tells me you and your man here are joining us for dinner?"

"I'm not really Blake's man," Harrison said, glancing at Blake.

Nathan raised a disdainful eyebrow. "No, when I say '*your man*,' it's just an Irish thing. You know, '*look at your man with the nice coat,*' '*is it your man I ask for to get a drink?* And are you not? Blake, I'm disappointed in you."

Blake narrowed his eyes. As he had predicted, Nathan could not have looked less disappointed if he had tried.

"Is Davina alright?" Harrison asked. "She seemed pretty upset earlier when I saw her."

Blake's lips thinned as he saw that patronising look on Nathan's face he had seen so many times during their relationship. "She's fine, thanks for asking, fella," he answered. "Nothing for you to worry yourself about." He tapped Harrison dismissively on the arm then carried on walking towards the hut, which was now just a few feet away from them. "Now, will we go? I'm fecking starved."

As he strode on ahead of them, Blake turned to Harrison and closed his eyes in silent frustration. "He's a character, I'll give him that." Harrison murmured.

"You are far too polite," Blake replied flatly.

When they reached the hut, Rupert was standing by the open door, waiting patiently for them.

"Evening!" he said, smiling warmly. "Come in, come in. Blake, nice to see you. Glad you could make it."

"Thanks," Blake said, stepping into the hut. "I appreciated the invite. Wow, you've certainly made it look nice."

"It's totally different to when I saw it this

morning," Harrison told him. "This big table wasn't here, for a start."

The table in the middle of the hut was just big enough to seat six people. Over it was a large white tablecloth with a few candles placed in the centre and silver cutlery was placed in size order in front of each chair.

"Where's Davina, Nathan?" Rupert asked once they were all inside. "I understand there was a bit of a fracas this morning?"

"You could say that," Nathan replied. "Your delightful brother has a lot to answer for, I'll tell you that for nothing. But I managed to calm her down. She's on her way down. She was after taking forever in the bathroom getting ready so I said I'd meet her down here."

"Must be quite a novelty for you," Blake said innocently. "To be with someone who actually takes longer getting ready than you."

Nathan chuckled dryly. "I forgot what a laugh a minute you were, Blakey."

"Oh, do you two know each other then?" Rupert asked, opening a bottle of wine from behind the mini bar.

"Sure. There's history," Nathan said, holding his glass up but not taking his eyes off Blake. "But that's all it is. Just history."

Bitterness ricocheted through Blake's body, but he merely smiled and said nothing.

"Polly will be joining us shortly," Rupert said glancing between Blake and Nathan. "She's just sorting out the menu for us tonight. If anybody has any allergies or anything, do let me know and I'll tell the kitchen?"

"Yeah, I'm vegan," Nathan said, taking a sip of his wine.

"Ah, yes. Don't worry, Davina mentioned that to Polly," Rupert said as he went around filling up everyone else's wine glasses.

Blake raised a disdainful eyebrow. "Vegan? Since when?"

"Since I started seeing Davina," Nathan replied, "We made a decision to cut out all meat, dairy, there's a lot of stuff I cut out once we became an item."

"You're not kidding," Blake replied, raising his glass to him.

Before Nathan could reply, the hut door slammed open and Davina and Polly rushed in.

"Polly?" Rupert said, looking at her concerned. "What's wrong?"

"Rupert, he's out there. The hooded man! We just saw him," Polly said urgently.

"What was he doing?" Blake asked, standing up. "Do you want me to go and have a look?"

"No, no, Blake," Rupert said firmly, indicating that Blake should sit down again. "I won't have my guests dealing with my problems."

"I'll phone the police," Davina said.

"What about your dinner?" Nathan asked her.

"There are more important things happening than stuffing your face, Nathan!" Davina snapped, before turning to Polly. "Lock this door behind me, just to be on the safe side. I'll be back when I've spoken to them."

"He'll be gone before they even get here," Polly said but she pulled out a set of keys from her pocket. "Be careful, Davina. He could be dangerous."

"It'll be fine. I'll go straight to the manor, and when I've spoken to them, I'll come straight back."

Davina left the hut and Polly closed the door behind her and locked the door.

"Right then," she said, apparently attempting to return everything to normal. "Sorry I'm late. Dinner won't be long."

"What are you all on about?" Nathan asked, frowning. Blake could tell he hated being the only person in the room who didn't know what was going on. "Hooded figure?"

"Oh, it's a long story, Nathan." Polly said, walking across the hut to the mini bar. "Don't you concern yourself with it. Can I get anybody a drink?"

"I've done the rounds with the wine, Polly," Rupert replied, taking his seat.

Polly nodded and knelt down behind the bar to make her own drink.

"But my wife has gone to phone the police. Why bother when we've got a detective sergeant sitting right here?" Nathan waved his wine glass in Blake's direction.

"Because I haven't got any jurisdiction, Nathan," Blake told him flatly. "I'm on holiday, away from where I usually work."

"Well, you used to work round here," Nathan replied.

"Yes, and then I moved," Blake snapped. "Remember?"

"Blake," Harrison said gently. "You don't need to do this now."

Blake glared furiously at Nathan, wondering why he possibly thought that he would be capable of spending this much time with him without attempting to bite his head off.

"Duncan is out there."

They all looked up at Rupert, who was standing in front of the window, staring out at the lake in front of the hut.

Polly popped her head out from underneath the bar. "He's not bloody fishing again, is he?"

Rupert nodded bitterly. "Despite how many times we've asked him not to, there he is." He stepped aside from the window so that they could all see. Blake craned his neck, glad of the distraction from Nathan. He could just make out Duncan with his back to them, sat in a small rowing boat in the centre of the lake, a fishing line out in front of him. He was wearing what looked like a deerstalker and a green jacket.

"Rather him than me in this cold," Harrison said.

"He knows how we feel about the fish in that lake," Polly fumed. "They're part of what makes these lakes so beautiful! He just doesn't care."

"I'll go and tell him," Rupert sighed. "Not that it'll make much difference, he's such a –"

But Polly suddenly gasped. "*Rupert*! He's there! The man with the hood, he's *there*!"

They all looked out of the window. Sure enough, there was the hooded figure. Whoever it was standing on the lake's edge, staring out at Duncan.

"Well," Rupert said. "At least now he can't tell us that we're making it up."

Blake stood up from his seat and walked across to the window. Duncan was now standing up in the boat, gesturing towards the hooded figure angrily.

"Who the *hell* is that?" Nathan exclaimed. "And what, you're saying he's after causing trouble round here?"

"We don't know who it is," Polly said nervously as they all watched what was happening. "But I'd like to see Duncan try and deal with him. One of them will be taught a lesson anyway."

"Well he's not going to do much when he can't even get to him," Blake reasoned. "Not when Duncan is right in the middle of-"

But then Blake stopped. What happened next rendered him incapable of speech.

The hooded figure took a step towards Duncan from the edge of the lake. Then another. And another. And then, impossibly, and without any visible means of support, they were standing on the surface of the lake. They all stared, bewildered at the sight before them through the window of the hut. Somehow, the hooded figure was walking on water.

"What the *hell?*" Rupert gasped.

"How is that possible?" Harrison asked quietly. "How is he-"

From the boat, Duncan seemed to go stiff, staring out at the figure who continued to walk across the lake towards him. He had been gesturing wildly, perhaps shouting at whoever it was to go away, but now he seemed paralysed with fear.

Nobody in the hut seemed capable of movement. Blake certainly could not take his eyes off what he was witnessing. It was absolutely impossible, but yet there he was, watching a human being walk across the surface of the lake.

At last, the hooded figure reached the boat. Slowly, they reached inside the cloak and pulled out what looked like a knife. Before any of the occupants of the hut could do anything, the figure made a stabbing motion at Duncan, who keeled over.

Polly let out a scream of horror and backed away from the window, coming to a rest behind the mini bar, her hands clasped to her mouth.

Again, the hooded figure stabbed the knife into

Duncan, this time pushing him backwards as he did so. Duncan stumbled over the side of the boat and landed in the lake, the sound of the heavy splash echoing round the grounds.

"Duncan!" yelled Rupert, rushing towards the hut door. He tried to pull it open, then turned to Polly. "You locked it, give me the keys."

"I'll-I'll do it," Polly stammered, standing up and hurrying across the hut, pushing Rupert out the way.

Her hands shaking, Polly pulled the keys from her pocket and attempted to unlock the door. In her panic, she dropped them on the floor and then had to find the right key again, but she finally unlocked the door to the hut and pulled it open.

They all ran outside and looked out over the water. Duncan was now lying in the lake, motionless. But he was alone. The hooded figure had completely disappeared.

CHAPTER
SEVEN

For a few seconds, there was pandemonium. Polly and Rupert were shouting at each other, crying out to Duncan, who remained motionless, lying in the lake, Nathan was crying out suggestions, asking where Davina was, and Harrison was just leant against the hut, his head in his hands, apparently unable to comprehend what he had just witnessed.

Amongst the confusion, Blake stared out at the lake, frantically trying to piece together what had just happened and how on earth it could have been possible. They had just witnessed a man being apparently stabbed to death, by someone who was able to walk on water and then disappear before their very eyes. None of it made the slightest bit of sense.

Rupert ran into the lake and began wading towards Duncan's lifeless body, crying out his name.

"That psycho is still running around somewhere," Nathan murmured. "We should get back in the hut."

"He's not going to show up now," Blake said quietly. "He just disappeared right in front us, what would be the point if he was just going to immediately reappear? I'm going to have a look around."

Harrison looked up. "But Blake, it's like Nathan said, he could be anywhere around here. You can't go looking for him on your own, he's got a knife."

"Ah, you've got a lot to learn about Blake, fella," Nathan said, somehow smirking, despite the situation. "A man's just walked on water. Blake Harte needs to know how he did it. You never could quite turn off from being the detective could you, Blakey?"

Blake glared at him but said nothing.

"There's a torch in the hut," Polly said, "The power went a few weeks ago and I left it in there. Hang on."

Rupert had now reached his brother and was pulling him towards the water's edge. "Someone ring an ambulance! He's not breathing!"

Nathan pulled his mobile out of his pocket and passed it to Rupert as Polly ran out of the hut, holding the torch out for Blake.

Blake took the torch and began walking towards the edge of the lake and shone the light into the centre of the pool, staring intently at the water. Harrison walked up behind him, glancing nervously at Duncan's body.

"Do you think he's dead?"

"I don't know."

"You do," Harrison said softly. "When Daniel died, you knew he was dead the second you saw him. You've said to me yourself, you've dealt with enough dead bodies in your old job back in the city to know when someone is dead."

Blake exhaled as he continued staring through the surface of the water.

"I don't *know* that he's dead," he said quietly, so that nobody other than Harrison would hear. "But what would be the point in all of that charade if you're just going to leave him wounded? The size of this mansion and its grounds, it would surely be easy enough to kill him without being seen, but no. Instead, whoever was under that hood wanted to make sure that plenty of people saw him do it. *Why*? You don't put on a performance like that if you don't have an audience."

Harrison thought for a moment, then nodded. "I suppose that makes sense. What are you looking for?"

"Well the only way I can think of for anybody to walk on water is for there to be some sort of support *under* the water. Like a path, or some platforms or something. There wasn't enough time to get rid of any, so they must still be here."

Harrison stared out at the centre of the lake, where just minutes ago the hooded figure had appeared to be standing. "And?"

"And there's nothing there." Blake frowned. "It's just *water*."

He picked up a few stones from the water's edge and threw them, one at a time, to where the figure had crossed the water. Each stone splashed loudly and then appeared to sink, undeterred on its journey to the bottom by any means of support for someone to stand on.

"So how the *hell* did he do it?"

Blake turned to where Nathan's voice was coming from, accidently shining the torch right in his eyes.

"Blake, for God's sake-" he snapped, holding his hands up to his face.

Blake put the torch to the ground, without apologising. "I don't know."

"And I bet that's winding you up good and proper, am I right?" Nathan asked lightly.

"Yes, that, and your voice," Blake replied, turning on his heels and walking away from them in the direction of where the hooded figure had first appeared.

Ignoring Nathan's retort to his back, Blake shone the torch in the direction of the bushes that was festooned around the large metal fence built along the back of the gardens. It didn't look like any of them had been disturbed by anybody climbing over the fence, and the wet mud near the lake didn't even have any footprints in it. To all intents and purposes, the hooded figure had levitated along the ground, across the water and then just vanished.

Blake's thoughts were interrupted by the sound of sirens in the distance.

"The police," Harrison said. "Blake, are they going to need you?"

"What do you mean?" Blake frowned, turning to him. "You mean, am I going to be one of the officers investigating?"

"Yeah."

Blake shook his head. "I'll have no jurisdiction. As far as the police will be concerned, I'm just another witness to what happened."

Nathan scoffed. "Not that *that'll* mean he doesn't stick his nose in and try to play Sherlock Holmes. Sorry fella," he slapped Harrison on the shoulder. "As of this moment, your little romantic getaway is over." He walked off back towards the hut as the sound of sirens got louder.

"Ignore him," Blake said, switching the off the torch.

"Maybe it's a good job that this happened," Harrison murmured. "Either way, looked like there was going to be a murder of *some* kind."

A few minutes later, Harrison and Blake were sat in the reception area of the hotel. After the arrival of an ambulance and two police cars, the few guests the mansion was housing had gathered in the entrance watching the emergency services with interest.

"I've never been on this side of the police investigations before," Blake said to him as he peered outside. "Ushered away from the scene and being told everything is in hand."

"Are the police going to want to speak to us?" Harrison asked him.

"I would think so," Blake replied. "After all, we were direct witnesses to-"

He stopped as he saw the two paramedics that had ran out of the ambulance when it had arrived, walking back towards their vehicle and climb into the front. Blake turned his head to Harrison as it began to drive away. "Direct witnesses to the murder."

"He's dead?" Harrison gasped, his eyes wide.

"The ambulance has driven away. Not a lot they can do to save a dead body."

Harrison exhaled and rested his head on the back of the sofa they were sat on. "Poor Rupert. Imagine watching your brother die like that. He must be in bits."

"Come on," Blake said. "We may as well get our interviews out of the way, see if there's anything we can do for the family." He stood up and began making his way through the crowd. "As if Rupert and Polly haven't got enough to deal with. And it's not going to get any easier for them."

Harrison ran to catch up with Blake as they made their way along the gravel path back towards the hut, where Rupert and Polly would be. "What do you mean?"

"I mean along with the fact that Rupert's brother has just been murdered, they've got his mother dying of cancer upstairs, she'll need informing, and the fact that they'll probably both be suspects."

"How can they be suspects?" Harrison asked him, confused. "They were both in the hut with us when it happened."

"Yes, but they both absolutely hated Duncan. Polly especially. She told me her whole family have done everything they can to make life hell for the Urquharts. I promise you, right now, her head will be all over the place, wondering if any of her own family would be capable of something like this because if I was in charge of the investigation, Polly's family would be my first port of call."

When they arrived at the lakes, the area was cordoned off with police tape. Duncan's body was being examined by a forensics team. One, covered head to toe in a white overcoat was standing over Duncan, taking pictures of the stab wounds on his body. Blake glanced at Harrison, who was staring at the body, exhaling slowly. Blake placed a hand on his shoulder and gave it a supportive squeeze. It was, after all, hardly the first time Harrison had had to witness scenes like this. The first time he and Blake had met, Harrison's boyfriend had been in a similar position and as it had turned out, he wasn't to be the first man in Harrison's life to meet a grisly fate.

"Excuse me, sir," a policeman said, walking across to them, with his arms outstretched in an attempt to block their view of Duncan's body. "But this area is out of bounds, as I'm sure you can imagine, the family is highly distressed at this time, so if you wouldn't mind-"

"Detective Sergeant Blake Harte," Blake said, pulling his wallet out of his pocket and opening it so that the officer could see his identification. "Don't worry, I'm not on duty, but I know full well the procedure. Well done by the way, quite right. The only reason we're here is that we were witness to the murder, so I figured you'd want to get interviewing us out of the way so you can get on with the investigation."

"Oh," the police officer said, his face dropping slightly as he read Blake's ID. "Well, that'll be up to our man in charge – I think he's interviewing the family at the moment but I'll be sure to tell him-"

"Blake?"

Blake turned to where the voice had come from and then smiled happily. "No way. I don't believe it!"

"You better believe it, sunshine," said Sally-Ann

Matthews, as she walked towards him from behind the hut, her arms outstretched. "What the hell are you doing here?"

The officer glanced at Sally, then wandered off, looking bemused.

"Would you believe this is the holiday I told you about?" Blake laughed, hugging her. "You remember Harrison?"

"Vaguely," Sally said, looking slightly sheepish. The last time she and Harrison had met, Sally had been very drunk. "How are you, Harrison?"

"Not too bad, thanks," Harrison said, smiling. "How come you're here though?"

"I told you, we're really not that far from where I used to live," Blake said. "A case like this, I should have realised you'd be one of the first on the scene. It's seriously so good to see you."

"Likewise," Sally said. "Though I wish it was under slightly better circumstances."

"Yeah, tell me about it." Blake sighed, scratching the back of his head. "I'm glad the family has you on the case. It's not going to be an easy one, Sally."

"Did you see what happened?"

"Yep."

"Is it true what the Urquharts are saying? Some hooded guy walking across the lake?"

Blake nodded grimly. "Yeah. Wish I could make some sense of it for you, but that is pretty much what happened. Anyway, as I was saying to your colleague,

I thought you might want to get interviewing us out of the way."

Sally glanced at the hut, looking slightly awkward. "It's not going to be me interviewing you Blake, someone else is probably going to be wanting to do that."

Blake frowned. "Who?"

The hut door slammed open and a rotund man with a bald head and a long brown jacket strode out. Blake's heart sank. The man's intense and disparaging mannerisms were just as present and annoying as Blake remembered. "You have *got* to be kidding me."

"Do you know him?" Harrison whispered.

"Unfortunately, yes," Blake replied, glaring at the pompous looking man. "That's Inspector Gresham. My old boss."

"And I'm sure he'll be absolutely thrilled to see you," Sally said, grinning at Blake's irritated expression.

"Matthews, I've interviewed the family," Gresham said, indicating the hut with a dismissive wave of his hand. "Not a lot of use, the brother is a bit of snivelling wreck at this stage. All I'm getting is this crap about a floating man. Were there any other witnesses?"

"Hello, Inspector Gresham," Blake said, with a vague attempt at politeness.

Gresham stared at Blake with a mixture of surprise and disdain. "Harte. What a surprise. I didn't expect to see you again."

"Likewise," Blake replied, giving Gresham a small nod. He wasn't sure whether he was still required to call his old boss '*sir*' or not. There was a long list of things he would certainly like to call him, but this was hardly the time to start reeling any of them off. "Myself and Harrison here were witness to what happened."

"I see," Gresham said, glancing at Harrison with an air of distaste. "Well, when the wife of the brother in there mentioned a Blake, I certainly didn't think it would be you I would be talking to. Still, I expect you to give me a slightly more helpful account of events. Matthews, if you'd like to talk to Mr Harte's-" he threw another disdainful look at Harrison "-*friend* here?"

"Certainly, Sir," Sally said, clearly trying not to laugh at Blake, who had his eyes narrowed in intense dislike at Gresham.

"You and me will take a walk this way, Harte," Gresham said, nodding his head along the path.

"Do you want to come with me, Harrison?" Sally said, leading Harrison around the police tape and towards the bushes, away from Duncan's body.

"See you later," Blake said. "Just tell Sally what you saw. It shouldn't take too long."

"No worries. Nice meeting you Mr Gresham."

Gresham grunted in reply and clicked his fingers towards the path, before striding off. Blake gritted his teeth and followed the old superior he had hated for so long back along the path.

CHAPTER
EIGHT

I f it weren't for the fact that Blake considered himself to be a consummate professional, he would have made the interview as difficult as he possibly could for Gresham. As it was, once he had managed to catch him up, and be in time with the long strides Gresham was taking, he knew that his hatred for his old inspector was second to finding out who had murdered Duncan Urquhart.

"So, how long have you been staying here?" Gresham said, pulling out his notepad along with a packet of cigarettes.

"We arrived last night," Blake said, eyeing the

menthol cigarette Gresham had put in his mouth. "Since when did you smoke?"

"Oh, I do smoke sometimes, certainly I do, sometimes." Gresham said, lighting it and inhaling deeply. It did nothing to help the cravings Blake had been feeling for the past couple of hours. "And you got friendly with the family pretty quickly?"

"You could say that," Blake replied, pulling his ecig out of his pocket and sucking on it, somewhat urgently. The lemon flavoured vapour hit the back of his throat weakly and unsatisfactorily. "My landlord knows Polly Urquhart and managed to get me a week here cheaply."

Gresham scribbled in his notebook. "I take it you've come here for a romantic getaway then?"

"It's not really a-"

"Did you manage to meet the victim?"

"Not directly, no. I saw him arguing with his brother. He didn't seem to be the nicest bloke in the world, if I'm honest."

Gresham put his cigarette in his mouth and inhaled hands free as he continued scribbling in his notebook. Blake had never been able to understand how he could read the scruffy handwriting he always used when conducting interviews. "What were they arguing about?"

"From what I understand, the Urquharts have only recently started this spa hotel business. Duncan hadn't been the most supportive, especially seeing as the business hadn't been going very well. To me, he seemed like a bit of a bully."

"Yes, well that was a word I always thought you used a bit too freely, so we'll discount that," Gresham said.

Blake nearly bit his tongue in half. A few years ago, Blake had complained to the superintendent about Gresham's behaviour towards a young suspect, where he done everything but used physical violence in an attempt to get a confession out of him. Gresham had somehow managed to get himself out of too much backlash over the situation, and, although Blake knew the superintendent would not have explicitly stated that Blake was the one who had made the complaint, he had made it clear that he did not trust or like Blake ever since.

"So you're basically saying that the family's relationship was strained?"

"Yes," Blake said tersely.

Gresham nodded, inhaling on his cigarette again whilst scribbling in the notebook. "Anybody else who you think might have had an issue with the victim? I'm sure you've thought it all through."

Again, Blake chose to ignore the thinly veiled jibe. "From what I've been told, he wasn't a man with many friends. In fact, if his behaviour that I witnessed was anything to go by, irrelevant as you think it might be, I would be very surprised if he had any friends at all."

"And the murder itself? What did you see?"

"Exactly what you've already been told by the family. This hooded figure, who had apparently been giving the Urquharts hassle for months, appeared on the edge of the lake, where the victim was in the centre of, fishing. He or she then, somehow, walked across the surface of the water and from what I saw managed to stab Duncan to death. We all ran outside but by the time we'd gotten out of the hut, he had completely vanished and the victim was just floating in the lake."

Gresham took one last drag on his cigarette, then discarded it carelessly into a bush, scribbling frantically. "Disappeared, complete with murder weapon presumably."

"I would think so. Have you arranged for any divers to go looking in the lake for any clues as to what might have happened?"

Gresham glared over his notepad. "Obviously I have begun arrangements for that, Harte, quite obviously. May I ask why you were in that hut in the first place? You've got a whole mansion here to wander about in."

"Harrison and me were invited to dinner with Rupert and Polly," Blake replied, leaning against a wall with his arms crossed. "There were also two other people with us."

Gresham finished scribbling in his notepad and put it back in his pocket, smirking delightedly. "Oh, yes, of course. I thought I recognised him. Your ex missus is here, isn't he? The one you *turned*."

Blake shook his head in disbelief. "I wonder why your officers don't like you. It really is a complete mystery to me. Are we done here?"

"For now, yes," Gresham replied, walking away back to the hut. "But don't go anywhere. Ex- officer of mine or not, you're a direct witness to the crime so I shall want to speak to you again. Until then, Mr Harte."

Blake watched him saunter arrogantly away, supressing a huge urge to throw a large stone from the ground at his retreating head. He leant against the wall again and exhaled as he tried to comprehend everything that had happened over the past twenty-four hours. He had not thought things could get any worse when he came face to face with Nathan, and yet here he was being interviewed by the boss who had tried so desperately to make his working life as difficult as possible, about a murder that despite the fact that Blake had witnessed first-hand, made absolutely no sense whatsoever.

"This is the worst holiday ever," he murmured to himself as he wandered back into the hotel.

A few hours later, Blake was sitting in the bar, cradling a glass of vodka and coke, far stronger than the one he had been drinking the night before. He glanced up as Rupert approached him, brandishing the vodka bottle.

"Refill, Blake? May as well take advantage of not having Duncan breathing down my neck anymore-" he cut himself off halfway through the sentence, possibly feeling like he had come across as harsh or heartless. "I didn't mean it like that. I don't know why I said that."

"Don't worry about it," Blake said, holding his glass up. "If anybody is entitled to say whatever they want, I would say it's you. You knew your brother better than anybody else after all."

Rupert filled Blake's glass up and sat down opposite him, looking exhausted. "Three hours I was talking to that inspector. Not exactly the most compassionate man I've ever met."

"No," Blake replied. "He isn't."

"Somebody said you used to work with him?" Rupert asked wearily. "I can't remember who, sorry."

Blake nodded. "We've got history. Anyway, that doesn't matter now. How are you? Stupid question, I know."

Rupert shook his head and looked up at the ceiling, perhaps in an attempt to stop himself from bursting into tears. "Numb. I think that's the only word I could possibly use at the minute. You could throw anything else at me right now and I don't think it would make one iota of difference to how I'm feeling."

Blake didn't reply, instead choosing to take a long

sip from his glass.

"Rupert was the most unreasonable, selfish and bullying bloke you could ever meet. I grew up with him, mostly in fear. He was always my parents' favourite. I don't care what they said. Duncan was the go-getter. The one out of the two of us they could trust to bring good reputation to the family name." He shrugged, looking slightly childish as he did so. "What was I supposed to do? I could only just get on with my own life whilst *Saint Duncan* did no wrong."

"Must have been difficult," Blake said softly. "Has anybody told your mother about what's happened yet?"

Before Rupert could reply, Polly walked into the bar, followed by Harrison.

"Finally," Blake said as Harrison sat down beside him. "Are you alright?"

"I'm alright, I think. After Sally was done interviewing me about what had happened, your old boss then pulled me aside and asked me exactly the same questions all over again. But whenever I told him anything, he was acting like he didn't believe me. He's *only* just let me go!"

Blake rolled his eyes. "Yeah, that sounds like Gresham. He thinks it's the best way to get the most honest account out of his witnesses, to try and chip them down till they think they're a suspect. Don't let him get to you, he's just an arsehole."

"You need to tell her, Rupert," Polly said

soothingly to Rupert as they pulled apart. "You can't let that inspector be the one to tell her."

Rupert ran his hands through his hair. "I can't. I can't do it, Polly. I can't be the one to tell her that Duncan-"

He stopped, emotion breaking through his voice.

"Do you mean your mum?" Blake asked.

Rupert nodded. "Polly, you'll have to-"

"Oh, no Rupert," Polly said pleadingly. "You can't expect me to. How I supposed to tell her that her son has been murdered? We don't even know who did it."

"Why don't *you* tell her, Blake?" Harrison asked, turning to him. "You're probably the most tactful person I've ever met."

Touched as Blake was by Harrison's accolade, he wished dearly that he had kept quiet, especially once he realised that both Rupert and Polly was looking hopefully at him. "I don't think it's really my place to-"

"Please, Blake," Rupert begged. "You're trained in this sort of thing, aren't you? Being a police officer? I hate to ask, but I…I love the woman dearly, but after all she's been through these past few years, what with her illnesses and the treatment, and my father's death. I can't tell her. I know that must sound terribly cowardly, but…please?"

Blake sighed as he glanced between Rupert and Polly then back at Harrison who had somewhat sunk into his chair, looking guilty and apologetic. "I have no jurisdiction in this case, you do realise that? If she's got any questions about the investigation, I genuinely will have no way of answering her."

"I'll show you to her room," Polly said, before turning to Rupert. "You get yourself to bed. Try and get some sleep. I'll be up in a minute. I think it might be best if we ask the rest of the guests to go home tomorrow, what do you think?"

"They'll all need interviewing before they can go anywhere," Blake told her as he passed Harrison the rest of his drink. If he was about to tell a very ill woman that her son had been brutally murdered, the last thing he wanted to appear was drunk, even if he wasn't on duty.

Rupert grasped Blake's hand as he stood up. "Thank you, Blake. I can't tell you how much I appreciate all you're doing for me."

Blake gave him a small smile, while at the same time wondering how he had managed to get himself into this situation. "It's no problem."

"Harrison, would you mind coming too?" Polly asked him once Rupert had left the bar. "I'm sure Patricia would appreciate a friendly face?"

Harrison stared up at her, looking horrified. "Me?"

"Why Harrison?" Blake asked her, equally as surprised.

"The way you rushed to help me this morning

when I was upset," Polly said, looking down fondly at Harrison, "I need someone to be there holding my hand. You don't mind do you?"

Harrison looked slightly lost for words for a moment, but he quickly seemed to pull himself together. "No, no of course not. If it's what you want?"

"Thank you," Polly said gratefully. "Well, let's get this over with shall we?"

CHAPTER
NINE

Patricia's room was at the top of the last flight of stairs and as they walked up the third sweeping staircase and past a sign that had the words *'STAFF ONLY'* written in large black letters, Harrison could not have felt more guilty for getting Blake into this position. He knew Blake would be as calm and as sensitive as the situation required, but it was not something he should have to have been doing.

"It's just down here," Polly told them.

The corridor they were now walking down looked very different to the rest of the hotel. While it was no less grand, more dust had been allowed to collect around the various picture frames that were hanging on the walls. As they walked silently along the dark corridor, Harrison noticed that the pictures on the wall were different to the ones downstairs in the reception area and the guests' hotel corridors. These pictures were of people, some were oil paintings, and others were photographs in sepia, black and white and just one or two in colour.

"Are these members of the family?" Blake asked, just as Harrison was about to ask the same question.

"That's right," Polly replied. She stopped and pointed to a large ornate frame near to the last door in the corridor. It contained an old photograph of a man and woman on their wedding day. The bride was a beautiful auburn haired woman with a beaming smile clutching the arm of the groom, a dashing older looking man with a beaming smile. "That's Patricia and Jeremy, Rupert's father, getting married. Look at her. So graceful and beautiful. I'm afraid it's a far cry from what she looks like now."

As they approached the door at the end of the corridor, Harrison leant forward and whispered "What's wrong with her?"

"Non Hodgkin's Lymphoma," Polly said quietly. "Nasty form of cancer, bless her. She's one of these unlucky ones that has just been absolutely plagued by illnesses all her life. Only in her sixties, but she's in a wheelchair and she's had a lot of chemo, which as you can imagine…" her voice drifted off as she indicated towards her own hair. Harrison nodded, feeling instant sympathy for the woman he was about to meet. Polly sighed as she knocked gently on the door. "What this will do to her, I dread to think. *Patricia*? It's Polly. I've got some people with me. Can we come in? We need to talk to you."

"Come in," said a raspy sounding voice behind the door

"Ready?" Polly asked Blake.

"Yeah."

The door creaked loudly as Polly slowly pushed it open. The room was dark and smelt slightly musty. "Patricia?"

In front of the window, with her back to them, was a frail looking woman in her wheelchair. She was wearing a white nightie, which flowed down to the floor. Her bald head shone in the moonlight from the window.

"Come in," she said without turning round. Her voice made her sound like she was incredibly out of breath and constantly thirsty. "Tell me, Polly. Why are the police here?"

Polly went to speak, but then looked at Blake helplessly.

Blake glanced at Patricia, appearing nervous before he took a deep breath and stepped forwards. "Mrs Urquhart? My name is Blake Harte, I'm a police officer."

Patricia turned her head weakly towards Blake.

"Forgive me for not standing."

Blake didn't seem sure how to respond to that. "I've been asked to speak to you. I'm afraid I've got some bad news."

"You people always do in my experience," Patricia wheezed, shifting herself around with some apparent difficulty so she could turn her wheelchair to face him.

Now she had turned, Harrison could make out her facial features better. She was looking at Blake with what looked like concern and trepidation, but Harrison couldn't help but wonder if this was an expression that had been on her skeletal face so regularly over the years, with doctors constantly giving her bad news about her health, that it was one that had become stuck permanently.

"Oh God," Polly said under her breath, looking down at the floor as she gripped Harrison's arm.

"It's about your son, Duncan," Blake said gently, kneeling down to her level. "I'm so very sorry to tell you this, but he was killed a few hours ago."

Harrison watched Patricia as she took in the news. Her worried expression hardly faltered, except her large eyes widened even further. "Dead?" she wheezed. "My Duncan? What do you mean? How can he be – Polly, what is this man talking about?"

"It's true, Patricia. I'm so sorry. He's been murdered," Polly said, her voice breaking as she gripped Harrison's hand arm tighter.

"*Murdered*?" Patricia exclaimed.

"He was attacked by someone wearing a long hood." Blake replied. "We couldn't see who it was."

Harrison was surprised to see Patricia was yet to burst into tears or show some signs of grief. Perhaps she had felt so much pain over the years, this was just another sort. Or maybe she was just in shock? Either way, Harrison could not take his eyes off the woman in front of him; he found her strangely fascinating. She looked a lot older than in her sixties, but beneath the wrinkles in her face and the wheezing in her voice, Harrison could just make out some life in Patricia. She looked to be somebody who had fought many battles throughout her life, but now she was a retired soldier, tired of fighting.

Without taking his eyes off Patricia, Harrison sat down on what he thought was a sturdy looking box behind him, but the lid gave way beneath him, sending his bottom half down through the box and his arms flying outwards to try and save himself crashing fully to the ground. Patricia and Blake turned to him, startled by the noise as Patricia's toiletry bag, which had been sat on top of a small chest of drawers beside Harrison fell to the ground and the contents spilled out.

"Oh, God! I'm so sorry," Harrison exclaimed. "I thought that box would hold me, let me just-"

"Who is this?" Patricia asked, watching Harrison scramble to pick up the contents of the toiletry bag.

"This is Harrison," Blake said, an apologetic air in his voice.

"Is he a policeman too? They're getting very young and careless aren't they?"

"No, I'm not an officer, sorry," Harrison replied hastily, as he put everything back into the toiletry bag as quickly but as carefully as possible. "I'm just here with Blake, that's all. Polly asked me to be here, I'm sorry, I didn't mean to-"

"Harrison and Blake have been incredibly supportive, Patricia," Polly said, taking the refilled toiletry bag from Harrison and rearranging it again. "To me *and* Rupert. I honestly don't know what I would have done without them."

Patricia went to reply, but instead began coughing loudly. This went on for a few seconds to be point where Blake stood up to offer her some assistance, but she waved a dismissive hand at him, so he sat down on the bed, watching her with concern in his eyes instead. "How is Rupert?" she wheezed at last. "Where is he?"

"He's gone to bed," Polly said, pulling a bottle of water out from a cupboard, before unscrewing the lid and passing it to Patricia. "He's in absolute bits. He loved Duncan, Patricia. You know that."

Patricia weakly nodded her head as she took a sip from the bottle. "He did. Foolishly, some might say."

Blake leant forwards towards her, his hands clasped together. "Patricia, I hope you don't think me insensitive when I say this, but you don't seem all that-"

"Surprised?" Patricia cut in.

"Well, yes."

"I'm not. Not really." She took another long sip from the bottle and closed her eyes, sighing as she gripped her side, looking like she was in pain. "Duncan didn't have many friends. Did you ever meet him?"

"Not directly, but I did see him," Blake replied, his tone giving nothing away as to his actual feelings about him.

"Then you'll know he was not the nicest of men," Patricia said, her tone weak but serious. "He couldn't treat another human being decently if his life depended on it. He hurt a lot of people in his lifetime. His father was just the same. I was almost relieved when *he* finally died, if anything just to give me some peace. Duncan was my son and I loved him very much. But am I surprised that he finally pushed somebody too far? No. I'm afraid not."

Blake glanced at Harrison, then looked thoughtful for a few moments. When he asked his next question, Harrison realised he had been pondering on whether to ask it at all.

"You're saying you could think of multiple people who could have done this?"

Again, Patricia began coughing, far more violently and this time, Blake had to move forwards in order to stop her falling out of the wheelchair. Finally, she leant back, clutching the bottle of water tightly and panted. Harrison could not have felt sorrier for her – she looked absolutely wretched, as if she was angrier at the pain than anything else.

"Yes," she whispered at last. "Though, Polly is who you should really be asking."

"She means my family," Polly said, as she gently poured water into Patricia's mouth. "Remember what I was saying about the trouble they caused at the wedding? Patricia was there. Despite all the pain, you were there, weren't you? To watch your son get married."

Patricia swallowed the water, then took hold of Polly's hand. "I wouldn't have missed it for the world."

"Did you tell Gresham about your family?" Blake asked her.

Polly shook her head, one eye still on Patricia. "I didn't think to. I was still in shock when he was interviewing me, and to be honest, I was more taken aback by how blunt he was being."

Blake groaned and rolled his eyes. "Yeah, that sounds like Gresham."

"You will find the person who did this to my son?" Patricia asked Blake, looking up at him pleadingly. "To be frank, I don't know how much longer I have left and the thought of dying whilst my son's death goes unpunished is just too much to bear."

Blake knelt down to Patricia's level again. "The thing is Patricia, I'm not in charge of this investigation. I'm actually just a guest at the manor, Harrison and me, we just happened to see it happen. There's police looking into what's happened though and they will find your son's killer and bring them to justice, I promise you that."

"You sound rehearsed," Patricia said, an unmistakable air of condescension in her voice, behind the wheezing. "The way you were talking just now didn't sound like you had a lot of faith. I want my son's killer *caught!*"

"Patricia," Harrison said nervously, stepping forwards. "The man in charge might not be that reliable, but there's another officer working on the case, and she's Blake's best friend who he used to work with. Blake knows his job and he wouldn't be that close to someone in the police if he thought they couldn't do it, would you Blake?"

Blake smiled. "No. I promise you, Patricia. Sergeant Matthews will make sure that everything goes the way it's supposed to."

"Well, we'll see, won't we?" Patricia replied crisply, turning her chair to the window again. From his own standpoint, Harrison could just about make out some figures in the dark by the lake where the murder had taken place. "I don't have a very high opinion of police, I'm afraid. Let's hope that you prove me wrong. Now, leave me alone, please."

Polly walked across the room and opened the door again. "I think we could all do with trying to get some rest. It's been one hell of a day."

Harrison found himself extremely keen to get out of the room. As he walked back out to the dark murky corridor again, he found himself with the unshakable feeling that something was wrong, but he had absolutely no idea what it was. As he and Blake made their way back towards the stairs, he decided that it must have merely been the fact that he had never seen anybody look as ill as Patricia had and it had unsettled him.

"I can't thank you enough, Blake," Polly said once they had reached the second floor again. "I'm sorry for asking you to do that."

"It's fine," Blake said. "I'm just sorry that she's going through everything that she is. I wouldn't wish any of that on my worst enemy."

Polly shook her head. "Well, I think I'll get to bed. No doubt those police will be interviewing Rupert and I all day, and then I've got to think how to get rid of the guests. We'll probably have to refund the money. This discount week was our last chance of getting this business off the ground and now…" She rubbed her eyes, looking tired and stressed. "I don't think I could say this to anybody else, but I can almost feel Duncan smirking at how all this has turned out. Anyway. Good night, and thanks again, both of you."

They bid Polly goodnight and watched her disappear down the corridor. When they heard the sound of a door closing in the direction Polly had gone, Blake leant against the stair bannisters and exhaled. "There's something very weird about all of this."

"What do you mean?" Harrison asked him.

Before Blake could reply, the main door to the reception opened and Sally-Ann stepped inside.

"Sally," called Blake, running down to the bottom of the stairs. "How's it all going?"

Sally looked at Blake and shook her head. "You know full well I'm not supposed to say anything to you Blake, you've got no jurisdiction. Gresham would kill me if he thought I was giving you any info."

"I know he would," Blake replied, and Harrison was surprised to see a small smile appearing at the side of his mouth. "Well, we've just been up to see the mother, Patricia Urquhart. Polly asked me to be the one who told her about her son's death."

"That's what I was just on my way to do," Sally said, giving Blake a swift smack on the arm, but she too then smiled. "You'd be all over this case if you were still with our force, wouldn't you?"

"He's all over it *now*," Harrison said, ignoring Blake's protests.

"Why am I not surprised?" Sally grinned, looking at Blake knowingly.

"None of it makes any sense, Sally," Blake replied. "If you want my honest opinion, Gresham is in way over his head here. And that's not even me claiming that I'd do any better. It's just all so weird."

"You want weird?" Sally sighed, glancing out of the window, possibly to see that her boss wasn't about to burst in. "I can give you weird."

"Why?" Blake said, frowning. "What's happened now?"

Sally glanced at Harrison, perhaps wondering whether to say what she had to say in front of him, but then said, quietly, "What did you say Urquhart was doing when that hooded figure killed him?"

"Fishing," Blake said. "He was in a small rowing boat, in the centre of the lake, fishing."

"I've just finished speaking to forensics," Sally continued. "They were looking at his stab wounds. According to them, the clotting around the wounds would indicate that he was stabbed at least four, five hours ago."

Harrison stared at her bemused. "What are you saying?"

Sally didn't reply, she just looked expectantly at Blake.

"She's saying," Blake murmured, "that Duncan Urquhart had already been stabbed to death when we saw him being attacked."

Harrison's eyes widened. "You mean-"

"Exactly. What we witnessed was the murder of a

man who was already dead."

CHAPTER
TEN

The next morning, Blake was lying on his front on top of his bed with a large sheet of paper in front of him that he had found at the bottom of one of the drawers in his room. He had spent most of the night tossing and turning with the bizarre details of the last few hours tirelessly going around his head until he had decided that trying to sleep any more was pointless. He had then mapped out all the facts he knew so far, including detailing out the apparent murder he had witnessed and how it had happened. As he had feared when he started however, anything solid that he could work with was still eluding him.

Since Sally had told him that Duncan had already been killed when Blake had seen him apparently standing up in a rowing boat and trying to defend himself against the spectral figure, Blake had hoped that because the situation was so impossible, something would stand out to him to make the rest of the illusion fall apart, but nothing he had written in front of him was being any help in him figuring out who had murdered Duncan, why or even how. If anything, his thoughts had become even murkier with a load of fruitless theories that led nowhere. Half of him was quite glad that he wasn't the officer in charge of the investigation, but then, as he stared aimlessly at the list of suspects he had written out in front of him, he realised that even when he was supposed to be on holiday, he clearly found it impossible to really let go and forget about his job, even in less extreme circumstances than this.

He was glad when he answered the door to find Harrison standing there, smiling.

"Morning," he said. "Did you sleep alright?"

"With a killer running around across lakes murdering people that are already dead? Yeah, like a log," Blake chuckled, holding the door open so Harrison could walk in.

"Me too," Harrison sighed, sitting down on the bed and looking down at the paper. "As if this family hasn't got enough to deal with anyway. Their mum being really ill, this hotel business going through the floor, and now this. I really feel for them."

"That's because you are a kind and caring person," Blake said, smiling warmly at him.

Harrison picked up the paper and began reading it. "Did you think of anything?"

Blake sighed. "No, not really. I can't get the fact that whoever was under that hood would have needed some sort of platform or something to stand on so that they could walk across the water, but then I've probably been watching too many episodes of *The Masked Magician*."

"So, do I start packing?" Harrison asked, looking up at Blake with an expression of disappointment. "Polly said she's going to be asking all the guests to leave today."

"Do you think that includes us?" Blake said, sitting on the bed beside him. "After all, she did say we're being a lot of help to her."

Harrison put the paper down and stared at Blake seriously. "You said you couldn't be part of the investigation, Blake. You said you don't have any jurisdiction."

"I don't, not really," Blake replied, rubbing his tired eyes.

"But Nathan was right, wasn't he?" Harrison murmured. "You've *got* to find out what's been happening."

Blake felt a jolt of annoyance at Nathan's name,

especially followed by the words *'was right.'* "Don't pay any attention to what Nathan said. Yes, I'll admit, I want to know who killed Duncan and why. But that's the part I've got no jurisdiction over. There's a team of officers investigating that."

"Led by someone who you used to work with, who you don't like," Harrison pointed out, grinning.

"Yes, but that's beside the point."

"Is it?"

Blake stared at Harrison. He had to admit that he had underestimated quite how perceptive Harrison was. "You know me better than I do myself, don't you?"

Harrison looked at the floor, embarrassed. "Sorry, I didn't mean to-"

"No, it's alright," Blake said, taking a hold of Harrison's hand. "I don't mind. It'll probably do me some good to be brought down a peg or two. You're right – I'd love to get one over on Gresham. He made my life hell when I was under him."

"So? What do we do?"

"*We?*"

Harrison picked up the piece of paper with all Blake's notes on and put it in front of them. "You not having any jurisdiction means that you're just a witness, right? Same as me and everybody else who was in that hut?"

"Right?"

"So that means that you and me are just normal

members of the public."

Blake frowned. "Where are you going with this?"

"There are two things I've always wanted in my life. One is for a guy to serenade me with some soppy love song. Don't look like that, it's true," he added when Blake raised an eyebrow. "And the other thing is I've always wondered what it would be like to be an amateur detective," Harrison replied. "This is my chance."

"Harrison," Blake said gently. "This isn't *Miss Marple* we're talking about here. Someone has been murdered, brutally. They were stabbed to death. This is *real* life. *Dangerous* real life."

Harrison sat himself up, looking like he was trying to make himself look as serious and adult as possible. "And don't you think that everything that has happened to me since we met has taught me all I need to know? I've had one boyfriend murdered by my parents, another jump off a church roof after murdering people himself. I'm not a child, Blake. I know it's dangerous."

"I'm not saying you're a child," Blake replied. "But, still – this isn't a game. There's absolutely no guarantee that whoever was under that hood won't try and attack somebody else."

"Then we should go home?" Harrison asked, standing up. "If it's not safe for us to be here, then the best thing would be for us to leave, right?"

Blake bit his lip, trying to think of a reply but he

was saved the trouble when there was another knock at the door.

"Come in?" Blake called.

The door opened and Sally walked in. "Polly Urquhart said this was your room," she glanced at Harrison and smiled coyly. "Not interrupting anything, am I?"

Blake rolled his eyes. "No. Are you here in an official capacity, officer?"

"I've been talking to Polly this morning," Sally said, taking her coat off and throwing it on a chair. "She's been telling me about her family and how they've been giving the Urquharts hassle all these years. She said she'd spoken to you about it. I was just about to go and speak to them."

"Good idea," Blake said, nodding. "And you're telling me this because?"

"I was wondering," Sally said innocently. "I wondered if you fancied a lift into town while I'm on my way there."

"I wasn't going into town."

"You are now. Get your coat on."

Blake looked at Harrison and was surprised to see he was grinning from ear to ear. "Sally, are you suggesting what I think you-"

"Look, Blake," Sally said firmly, sitting on the bed. "It's as simple as this. You know just about as much about this case as we do, if not more. If you happened to be on your way to see Polly's family, and

I just happened to turn up to interview them while you were there-"

"Sally, listen to me. I am no longer your superior officer, you know that. Gresham would have a fit if he knew I was helping you investigate. It's not even-"

"And Gresham's not here is he?" Sally pressed. "He's talking to the guests downstairs, lording it about the way he always does. I know you're dying to get involved in this one, Blake."

"That's what *I* said," Harrison added.

"So, come with me. Me and you, one last interview together. Come on, Blake. Where's that detective I once knew who wouldn't rest until he'd found his culprit?"

Blake looked between Harrison and Polly and sighed. "Fine, I'll go with you. But I'm not saying anything – I'm just going as your number two. That's all."

"Fine," Sally said, smirking to herself. "I'm sure you'll be able to keep quiet."

"Shall I just stay here?" Harrison asked, as Blake picked his coat up.

Sally glanced between the two of them. "I'll wait for you outside."

Blake watched her leave and then sat down on the bed again. "Harrison, I shouldn't even be going. I can't let you go too."

Harrison nodded. "I know, it's fine." Blake could tell he was extremely disappointed.

"Look. We don't even know if we're staying. Why don't you go and talk to Polly and find out what she wants us to do?"

Again, Harrison nodded. But as Blake stood up and walked towards the door, he said, "Nathan *was* right though wasn't he? This week came to an end as soon as that murder happened."

"Of course it did, Harrison. Someone lost their life!" Blake replied, staring at him, confused.

"That's not what I meant," Harrison said, before standing up and walking out the room without another word.

"Well? What do you *think* he meant?" Sally asked him as she climbed into the driver's seat and started the car.

"I have no idea," Blake replied hotly. "I mean, Harrison isn't really one for metaphors and double meanings. So I don't actually have a clue."

"Blake, you know I love you, yes?" Sally said, as they pulled out of the car park and towards the main road.

"Yes?"

"Good. You really are an absolute tit sometimes, aren't you?"

Blake rolled his eyes. "Why?"

"He means that your time together came to an end when that murder happened. The romantic little getaway. As in you would drop anything if it meant you getting to the bottom of some case. It's *always* been your way, Blake. You know when you were still at Sale, the one thing that everybody said about you? *'The best officer we've got, great with suspects, great with victims, and every single night, goes home to sleep with Scotland Yard.'"*

"Catchy," Blake muttered sarcastically.

"You know what I mean."

"You're the one who asked me to come with you!"

"I know, but don't you see what he was hinting at when he was asking you to play Sherlock to his Doctor Watson?" Sally asked. "He wants to be a part of your life."

"And I want to be a part of his," Blake replied, annoyed. "But…" He paused and rested his head on the window, staring out at the countryside flying past. He had forgotten how quickly Sally drove when she was in interrogation mode.

"But what?"

"Ever since I met Harrison, his whole life has been turned upside down. And you know as well as I do how difficult being in a relationship with a copper can be sometimes. I mean, there's got to be some reason Nathan went for a safer option."

"Oh, come on, Blake," Sally tutted, swinging the steering wheel round to take them round a sharp bend in the road. "You can't start blaming yourself for Nathan cheating on you, that's ridiculous."

"I'm not. But what I'm saying is ours isn't a job of guarantees. When I go to work every day, there's not a one hundred percent chance I'm coming home that night. Or the night after. Do you get what I mean?"

Sally looked at him, sympathy in her eyes. "Of course I do. But come on, Blake. You live in Harmschapel. It's a village the size of a matchbox. Compared to where you used to be, it's a lot safer."

"I know, but you do realise that the two murder cases I've been in charge of in Harmschapel have both involved Harrison in some capacity? And one of them nearly killed both of us."

"Yes, and Mrs Hutchins could get knocked down by a bus on her way to her shift at the local supermarket," reasoned Sally. "I get that seeing Nathan again has raked up a lot of confusing feelings, but you've got to get your head straight. You said Harrison had told you that he needed to come to terms with a few things. Maybe he's not the only one."

Blake stayed silent.

Before long, Sally was pulling the car up to an isolated house in the middle of the countryside. Blake had been surprised when Sally had driven the car straight through some of the surrounding villages, but as it turned out, this was not Sally's first visit to the Lomax house.

"We're well aware of the Lomaxs," she said to Blake as the car came to a stop in the large yard outside the house. "Remember, the Urquharts think that one of them is this hooded figure. They're always delighted to see me."

She grinned as she pulled the keys out of the ignition and climbed out of the car.

"Do you have your ID with you?" she asked him as they walked along the gravel path towards the house.

"Yes, it's in my wallet. Not that it matters – I'm not the one who's going to be asking the questions, remember?"

Sally threw him another cheeky smile. "Then, why'd you bring it with you, *Detective*?"

Before Blake could reply, the loud sound of a steam train's whistle blasted out around them, causing Blake to jump about a foot in the air. Sally laughed as he caught his breath and waited for his heartbeat to return to its normal speed.

"Oh, did I forget to mention?" she added lightly. "They've got motion sensors to let them know when they've got visitors. I did exactly the same as you when I first came here."

"A train whistle?" Blake panted, clutching his chest.

Sally shrugged. "Some people have security lights, some people who are crazy into trains like the Lomaxs have the sound of a train whistle. Apparently it's *The*

Flying Scotsman."

Blake shook his head in disbelief as they arrived at the front door of the house. "What sound does the doorbell make? The theme tune to *Thomas the Tank Engine?"*

But before he could press the bell to find out, a sharp voice called out from behind them.

"What the *hell* do you lot want from us again?"

They turned to see an angry looking old man standing in the doorway to a large shed on the other side of the yard. He had a grey beard and similar coloured short hair and was wearing a white vest, covered in, what looked like, grease and oil.

"Morning, Lionel," Sally said cheerfully, walking towards him and holding out her ID. "You remember me, Sergeant Sally Matthews, this is my colleague, Detective Sergeant Blake Harte."

She subtly nudged Blake in the ribs, signalling him to produce his own identification from his wallet.

"I don't give a monkeys who you are," the old man replied, grumpily. "Just tell me what your business is and push off. If it's those toffee nosed Urquharts again, grassing us up about something or other, then you can just turn right round and drive off again. I've got nothing to tell you."

He turned around and walked back into the shed. Sally raised an eyebrow at Blake and followed Lionel through the door. Blake was surprised that Lionel appeared to have no idea as to why they wanted to speak to him, then had to remind himself that he was not in Harmschapel, and news of the murder would probably not have reached him, especially in a secluded area like this.

"It is to do with the Urquharts actually," Sally said as she walked into the large shed. "But I'm afraid this is a bit more serious than a bit of alleged vandalism."

As Blake followed Sally through the large wooden doors, he was surprised to see that the shed was more like a large workshop. All around were large sheets of scrap steel, toolboxes, workbenches, and placed precariously on the walls around were various parts of what Blake could only assume to be old steam engines. Most impressive of all was the huge model railway set in the centre of the workshop, which had various model trains and wagons running around it.

"Whatever it is, it had nothing to do with any of us," Lionel grunted, peering in a toolbox with his back to them.

"We're here investigating a murder, Mr Lomax." Blake found himself saying, before closing his eyes regretfully. It had been completely automatic.

Lionel stood up straight and turned to face them, looking stunned. "A *murder*?"

"Duncan Urquhart was killed last night," Sally replied, staring at Lionel seriously. "You might remember we've had cause to ask you about a hooded figure that's been harassing the Urquharts over the past year or so?"

Lionel nodded, his eyes still wide.

"Well, I'm sorry to say that whoever it was rather stepped up their game," Sally continued. "Now, considering the, I think it's fair to say, hardly secret problems between your family and the Urquharts, the fact that you and your son turned up at a wedding at the Urquhart manor and had to be physically removed by police for an unprovoked attack on the family, it shouldn't be very difficult for you to work out why we're here."

"So, any trouble that goes on for that family and we're automatically involved, is that it?" Lionel snapped, throwing the wrench he was holding into the metal toolbox with a large clang.

Sally continued her calm gaze at him. "Where were you last night between the hours of seven and eleven PM?"

"I was here," Lionel replied. "And so was Micky."

"Where *is* your son at the minute?" Sally asked him.

"Why?" Lionel snapped. "Want to throw more accusations at him? Lock him up again for something else he didn't do?"

"I take it that young Mr Lomax is a regular of yours?" Blake asked Sally, crossing his arms.

"He is indeed," Sally replied, not taking her eyes off Lionel. "What have we had him for in the past, Lionel? Vandalism? GBH? Theft?"

"You'd blame him for other countries wars if you got the chance," Lionel grunted. "Anyway, he's not here."

"Nah, it's alright, Dad. I've got nothin' to hide."

They all turned to the doorway where a cocky young man in a tracksuit and baseball cap was standing with his hands in his pockets and a lit cigarette between his lips.

"You don't need to tell them anything, son," Lionel told him as he strode arrogantly into the workshop. "You've done nothing wrong."

"Thought it had been a while since you showed your pretty face," Micky said, winking at Sally whilst deliberately looking her up and down. "You come to put those cuffs on me, again darlin'? If you wanna go for a date sometime, you only had to ask."

Blake glanced at Sally, who merely smirked at Micky. "Where were you last night, Michael?"

Micky threw himself onto a revolving chair on the other side of the workshop and dragged his feet along the ground so that he rolled towards them. "Don't think I remember."

"No?" Sally remarked lightly. "Well, that's a shame because we're here because of a murder enquiry, so do I take it we should be putting you right on top of the suspects list?"

Despite his bravado, Micky's cocksure facial expressions visibly faltered to the point where Blake had to suppress a chuckle. Like so many lads his own age that Blake had dealt with in the past, there was a line that Micky clearly felt he should not go over whilst trying to wind the police up and apparently being connected to a murder was that line. "Murder? Who's been murdered?"

"Duncan Urquhart," Blake replied. "Last night. So, do you want to think about your answer again?"

Micky glared at Blake briefly before glancing at his father. "I was here all night from seven."

"Anyone else who can verify that?"

Micky smirked again. "Yeah. You lot probably can." He pulled up the leg on his tracksuits to reveal an electronic tag strapped around his ankle.

"When did you get that?" Sally asked, looking at him surprised.

"After the last time you lot unfairly arrested me," Micky replied, sitting up again and spinning around slowly in the chair. "Or don't the other pigs talk to you?"

"They do," Sally said sweetly. "But I tend to only find out about people actually worth my time keeping an eye on. Not little kids trying to act the big man."

Micky looked sullenly back at her, clearly insulted, but said nothing more. Again, Blake had to stop himself from laughing.

"What about your wife, Lionel?" Sally asked. "Where is she?"

"Visiting her mother," Lionel replied. "I have train ticket receipts inside if you don't believe me. She took the 16:12 service to Lowestoft last night. I dropped her at the station myself."

"You're quite keen on trains, I understand, Mr Lomax?" Blake asked, indicating the impressive model railway in the centre of the workshop.

"Is that a crime now, as well?" Lionel snapped.

"Not at all. But from what I've gathered, your family used to own a steam railway where the Urquhart manor now is?"

"You're looking at it," Lionel replied.

"Is this a representation of the railway?" Blake asked, raising his eyebrows. "Wow. I have to say, I'm very impressed. This is really detailed."

"Right down to the trees on the side of the line," Lionel said, his defence dropping slightly from Blake's compliments. "All the different points and sidings, tunnels. It wasn't the main line, but my grandparents were very proud of it."

"I bet," Blake said. "It must have been horrible for your family to lose it all, just like that."

"Well, it was over time, but yes," Lionel replied, watching the model trains go around the tracks wistfully. "I would have loved to have the opportunity to be able to run my own railway, but I was only young when that manor was built."

He pointed towards a station with only the one track leading towards it. "That's where the manor is now. You can see the two lakes just a bit further on from the station. End of the line. The engines would turn round and then take any visitors back up the track again."

"But this huge rivalry between the families still remains?" Blake asked him, studying the area of the line where the Manor of the Lakes now stood.

"Detective, the Urquharts destroyed my family's heritage," Lionel replied, looking angry again. "These sort of things, they're never forgotten. There's resentment and bad blood that'll last longer than this railway managed."

"Your own daughter has married an Urquhart," Blake told him. "From what I've seen Polly and Rupert are very happy together. Is that not enough?"

Micky laughed and spun round on the chair again. "Don't talk to him about Polly."

"She left this family when she walked down that aisle," Lionel said firmly. "Nothing more to say."

There was a few moments silence, then Sally began telling the Lomaxs that they would need to be spoken to again. While she was doing this, Blake watched one of the trains going around the model track and then glanced around the workshop again. He wandered over towards the large steel plates leaning against one of the far walls and toyed with it to gauge its weight, thinking intently. Sally tapped him on the shoulder and they began walking back towards the car.

"Is that bloody steam whistle going to go off aga-" Blake began, before giving another startled jump as the high pitched whistle rang out across the yard again.

Once they were back inside the car, Sally turned to him. "What do you think?"

Blake shook his head, trying to piece what he knew so far together. "I feel like there's answers staring me in the face and I'm not seeing them."

"Those sheets of steel he's got in that workshop," Sally began. "They looked like-"

"Like they could hold the weight of somebody standing on top of them?" Blake sighed. "I know, that's exactly what I thought. It'd be easy enough to set up, maybe with a bit of inside help. I dunno, on top of some poles or something and then he just walks across. Except there wasn't any supports for that hooded man to walk across when I looked in that lake a few minutes after the murder. And even if there were, why? That's what I don't get about any of this, why would you go to the trouble of setting up some massive illusion like that where you know you've got people watching you when it would be far easier to just stab in the back in his room or something?"

Sally started the car and they began to drive out of the yard. "It could have been Lionel underneath that hood. If Micky was tagged and their mother, who's a piece of work as well to be honest, was out of town, if it was any of them, it would have to be Lionel?"

Blake leant back in his seat and shook his head.

"He's not tall enough, Sal. I was staring at whoever it was, they towered over Duncan, even when he was stood up. Lionel's only about five foot eight, if that."

"So, say we discount the Lomaxs for a minute," Sally said as they pulled out onto the main road. "Who else is there that would want to cause harm to Duncan?"

"Well, his mother reckons just about anyone he came into contact with," Blake answered, pulling his ecig out of his pocket. "But the people who were in that hut with us-"

Blake stopped, his eyes wide.

"What?" Sally asked, frowning at him.

"Oh my God," Blake murmured. "The one person I completely forgot about. She wasn't even in the hut with us when it happened."

"Who?"

"Davina," Blake replied. "Nathan's wife."

CHAPTER
ELEVEN

Harrison wandered around the grounds of the manor, feeling bored and miserable. His suggestion to Blake that they investigate what had happened to Duncan had not been one he had intended for Blake to take entirely seriously, but all the same it had annoyed him when Blake had dismissed the idea so quickly.

As he reached the hut, the lake where Duncan had been murdered shimmered as a strong gust of wind blew over the surface of the water, creating a series of small waves that lapped over the water's edge. Harrison sighed and turned his back to face the other lake behind the hut. If he was going to sit and stare, wistfully over a body of water, he decided he would rather it was one that had not been the scene of a murder.

He sat down and pulled his legs up to his chin. A swan flew down to the lake and glided across the surface before coming to a stop somewhere in the middle.

Was he kidding himself? Was it realistic that he and Blake could actually ever make it work? Before he had met Nathan, Harrison might have thought so, but Nathan, cocky and irritating as he might be, was also confident, good looking, and witty. Although Harrison had never thought of himself as an unattractive person, his self-confidence always seemed to hold him back. There was surely only so long Blake would be able to handle that, Harrison's deep rooted feelings that he wasn't good enough, before it started to cause problems in their relationship.

There was no telling how long Blake would be, and Harrison still needed to find Polly and ask whether she wanted them to stay or not. He decided to get that particular line of questioning over and done with. At least if Polly said that it would be best if they left, he and Blake might be able to salvage some more time together somewhere else before they both had to return to Harmschapel.

He stood up and was just about to start walking back towards the mansion when he heard two angry voices coming towards him.

"...don't see anything wrong in me asking what the hell is up with you?"

"I've told you, there's absolutely nothing wrong. Seriously, can you just get off my case?"

It was Nathan and Davina. They were walking straight towards him and Nathan was the last person Harrison wanted to see at that moment. He ducked out of sight behind a hedge, hoping they would keep on walking, but to his dismay, they were heading straight towards the hut.

"I'm your husband, for God's sake! Will you stop being so defensive? I'm actually worried about you!"

"So concerned that you've been talking non-stop about that bloody policeman since he arrived here?"

"No I haven't."

They were now so close that Harrison had to lie down on the floor behind the hedge to avoid being seen. Through the hedge, he could see Davina trying to get into the hut.

"Oh, bloody thing's locked!"

"Good!" Nathan said, crossing his arms and standing in her way. "So, tell me what's wrong. You've been acting like a bear with a sore head since yesterday."

"Is it any wonder?"

"And don't try and tell me that it's just to do with Blake," Nathan replied sharply. "Not that you've got anything to worry about."

"No," Davina said sarcastically. "Course I haven't."

Nathan rolled his eyes and then raised his eyebrows expectantly for her to continue.

"In case you've forgotten, there was a murder here yesterday."

"Yeah, I know that. I saw it happen, remember? You didn't. And the victim was somebody who's treated you like dirt since you started working here."

"I know," Davina said, sighing.

"Then, what's your problem?"

Davina glanced around them. Harrison had to flatten his whole body against the floor to avoid direct eye contact with her, but it was too late now for him to try and get away.

"You do love me, don't you?" Davina asked quietly.

"You don't even need to ask that question," Nathan replied, frowning.

"Don't I?"

"Oh for the love of -" Nathan began to walk off, but Davina grabbed his arm and pulled him back.

"No, wait," she pleaded. "*Listen* to me."

Harrison's legs were starting to hurt from the position he had landed in but he daren't move in case he attracted attention to himself. Davina took a deep breath. It seemed there was something she wanted to say, but she did not know how to word it.

"I've done something," she murmured. "But I

only did it because I want me and you to work. I did it for us."

Nathan stared at her confused. "What are you talking about?"

Davina looked down at the ground, shuffling uncomfortably. "I didn't feel like I had a lot of choice, and I'm not blaming you for that, I promise. You know the money problems we've been having? I got offered a solution, and I took it. But-"

She stopped and stared behind Nathan, frowning.

"*What?*" Nathan pressed, trying to catch her eye again. "What have you done?"

"Something's wrong," Davina said, ignoring him. "Look, an ambulance has just turned up!"

Harrison craned his neck as discreetly as he could, but before he could take a proper look, Davina had already begun running back towards the mansion, with Nathan in hot pursuit. Standing up, Harrison could see that Davina was right – there was an ambulance roaring its way through the empty car park, towards the mansion, its blue lights flashing and siren screaming.

Holding back just far enough so Nathan and Davina would not suspect him being so nearby, Harrison jogged back to the mansion in time to see the doors flying open and Patricia Urquhart being wheeled out on a stretcher, convulsing wildly.

"What's happened to her?" Nathan asked Polly as she ran out of the doors to the reception area and towards the ambulance.

Before Polly could answer, Inspector Gresham stepped outside, watching the paramedics putting Patricia into the ambulance with an expression of annoyance on his face. "She started having a fit just as I was interviewing her."

"It's a *seizure*, you stupid man!" Polly snapped at him. "She was having a *seizure*. It's a symptom of her illness and it can happen at any time."

"Is she going to be alright?" Harrison asked.

Nathan and Davina turned round, surprised to see Harrison standing right behind them. Davina maintained her stare, which Harrison tried his hardest to avoid.

"I don't know," Polly said. "It's happened before, but not to this level, it was a very intense one and as you can see, she's still shaking."

"*Mother!*" cried another voice from inside the mansion, before Rupert came running out. "Is she alright? Is it another fit? I have to go with her!"

Polly gripped his wrists and talked calmly to him. "She is going to be *fine*, Rupert. I'm going with her, there's nothing you'll be able to do. There's things to sort out here. The Inspector will want to speak to you. I will call you from the hospital."

"I can't lose her too," Rupert whimpered, looking on the verge of tears. "I just *can't!*"

"She'll be absolutely fine, fella," Nathan said, clapping Rupert on the shoulder. "She's in the best hands." Even with the severity of the situation, Harrison could not help but think how exceptionally irritating he found Nathan. He was struggling to see what could ever have attracted Blake to him in the first place.

"Yes, I'd rather like to speak to you, Mr Urquhart. There's a few things I'd like to clarify about your relationship with your brother, if you don't mind?"

"I've told you everything I know, please!" Rupert cried, as Polly kissed him briefly and ran towards the ambulance. "My mother is being taken away in the back of an ambulance. She's extremely unwell! Can we not do this later?"

"I'm inclined to agree with the gentleman here," Gresham replied carelessly, nodding his head at Nathan. "She's in the best possible hands. But if you don't mind, I've got a murder to investigate. Your wife will call you from the hospital, so if you would?"

He pointed towards the entrance to the manor and raised his eyebrows pompously. Harrison could quite easily see why Blake had hated working under him so much. He seemed to have very little compassion for anybody, especially when compared to Blake.

Rupert sighed, running his hands through his hair before turning round and striding through the main doors, pursued by Gresham, leaving Davina, Nathan, and Harrison standing in silence as the sound of the ambulance sirens faded away in the distance.

"What were you going to tell me?" Nathan asked Davina at last, before turning to Harrison. "Would you mind pushing off, fella? We're trying to have a private discussion here."

"It doesn't matter," Davina murmured, shaking her head, and running towards the door of the mansion.

"Davina, we were talking," Nathan said hotly.

"I said it doesn't *matter,* Nathan!" she exclaimed. She swung the door open and disappeared inside, slamming the door behind her.

Nathan let out a moan and turned to Harrison angrily. "What are you lurking about here for? Blake got bored of you already, has he?"

Harrison wished he could argue the opposite, but he was not entirely sure he truthfully could. "He's gone off with one of the police officers, actually. He'll be back soon."

Nathan smirked knowingly. "What did I tell you? He won't be able to rest now until he works out who did it. A word of advice now it's just you and me, fella. Don't ever think you'll take priority in Blake's life. The only way you'll ever hold his full attention is if you go out and murder somebody. Take it from me, relationships are not Blake's strong point."

Harrison felt a surge of anger go through him, fully aware that Nathan was getting to him as much as he clearly meant to. "It doesn't look like yours is going all that well. I overheard what you two were talking about back there. She's got secrets. What's happened? Is it something to do with Duncan's murder?"

Nathan stared at him for a moment, then rolled his eyes dismissively. "Got quite the imagination there, haven't you fella? I think I'd know if my own wife was involved in a murder, don't you?"

"She was the only one who wasn't in that hut when we saw the murder happen," Harrison continued, attempting to convey an air of superiority, but not entirely convinced it was working.

"I didn't see Mariah Carey in there either, have you accounted for her movements the other night?" He took a step towards Harrison and leant forwards. "Stop trying to be impress Blake. It'll never happen. Just move on with your life. You're wasting your time. I hate to break it to you, fella, but since he saw me again, haven't you noticed that Blake has barely paid you any attention? There's a reason for that. Try working that out before you start trying to-"

"Is there a problem here?"

Both Harrison and Nathan's heads quickly turned to where the voice had come from. Blake and Sally were striding towards them.

"No problems at all, Blakey. Me and Harrison here were just having a nice little chat, isn't that right, fella?"

Harrison didn't answer. He just looked down at the ground, embarrassed that, once again, Blake had to jump to his defence.

"Well, you folks be having yourselves a good evening." Nathan threw one last smirk at Harrison then disappeared into the mansion.

"What was that about?" Blake asked, his eyes on the door that Nathan had just slammed behind him.

"Oh, nothing much," Harrison said, shrugging. "How did it go with the Lomaxs?"

Blake glanced at Sally. "Good question. We're not sure."

"It's been pretty eventful here, since you've been gone," Harrison told him, glad that subject of Nathan seemed to be behind them. "Patricia Urquhart got taken away in an ambulance."

Sally raised her eyebrows. "Is that the mother? She's got cancer, right? What happened?"

Before Harrison could reply, the door to the manor burst open again and Inspector Gresham strode out, glaring at Blake and Sally.

"And where the *hell* have you been?" he snapped.

"I've been speaking to the Lomaxs, Sir," Sally replied, smiling sweetly at her boss. "You know, Polly Urquhart's family who have been reported for giving the Urquharts so much trouble."

"*And?*" Gresham exclaimed sharply, a small vein appearing on the side of his head.

"We'll have to check out their stories for sure, but

it looks to me like none of them were anywhere near this manor last night."

Gresham's eyes landed on Blake. "And what were *you* doing with my sergeant?"

"You haven't asked me that question since that Christmas party a few years ago," Blake replied, glancing at Sally who snorted with laughter.

"*Don't* take the micky. Answer the question!" Gresham retorted angrily.

"I was giving him a lift, Sir," Sally replied. "I saw Blake walking back from one of the villages, and I offered him a lift."

"Sergeant Matthews, that car is not to be used for you to run a personal *taxi* service!" Gresham exclaimed, the vein in his head throbbing furiously. He stormed towards Blake, looking up at him angrily with his hands on his hips. "And as for *you* Harte, keep your nose out of my investigation. Am I clear? What are you even still *doing* here anyway?"

"I'm on holiday," Blake replied innocently, looking down at Gresham with some amusement. From Harrison's perspective, the size difference between the two men looked fairly comical, especially with how annoyed Gresham was.

Gresham glared at Blake. "I know your game, Harte. You haven't lost a single bit of that superiority complex."

"I don't –"

"And for your *information,*" Gresham

interrupted. "I am extremely close to making an arrest and putting this whole sorry affair to bed."

"An arrest?" Sally repeated. "Who?"

"Need to know, Matthews. *Need to know*," Gresham replied smugly, tapping his nose, before returning his glare back to Blake, who continued looking down at the smaller man with a deadpan expression on his face. "So, as you can *see* Harte, your services are in no way required. Matthews, with me, let's *go!*" He pushed past Blake and pointed towards the car park, striding away with his coat flapping behind him in the breeze. Sally glanced at Blake with an exasperated look and followed her angry little boss to the car.

"Who's he going to arrest?" Harrison asked, as they watched the police car drive away.

"God only knows," Blake muttered. "But whoever it is, I bet they didn't do it. I wouldn't put it past Gresham to arrest someone who's got absolutely nothing to do with it whatsoever." He turned back to Harrison and smiled. "So, what have you been doing since I've been gone?"

Harrison shrugged. "Not much."

"Arguing with my ex?" Blake asked, putting his hand on Harrison's shoulder.

"It was more him doing the arguing," Harrison replied, as Blake led him towards the door of the mansion. "And it wasn't just me he was having words with."

"What do you mean?"

"Davina. I overheard them talking. I don't know what they were arguing about, but Davina was saying that she'd done something, and she looked like, whatever it was, it was something bad. But before she could say what it was, the ambulance came to pick up Mrs Urquhart. Apparently she'd had some sort of fit."

They walked inside the mansion and towards the stairs. "Is she going to be alright?" Blake asked.

"I don't know. Polly went with her."

"And Rupert didn't?"

"No. I think he wanted to, but Polly went instead, she said she'd call him from the hospital."

Blake frowned as they reached their corridor. "Did she?"

As he thoughtfully unlocked his room, he opened the door wide and held it open.

"Did you mean it when you said you thought we could solve this together?"

Harrison looked at the floor, putting his hands in his pockets. "Yeah, of course. But you're right, it is dangerous. And I probably wouldn't be much help to you anyway, you're a detective, you've been doing this sort of thing for years, I'm an ex farmer who now works in a shop."

"Yes I am and yes you are," Blake said, taking hold of Harrison's hand and leading him into his room. "But, you've also seen exactly the same as me. You're a bright guy. You've got as much chance of working this out as me."

Harrison gave him a small smile. "Thanks."

"But," Blake said, "I don't want to talk about that right now."

"Then what do you want to-"

But Harrison's words were suddenly supressed. The next second, Harrison could not even remember what those words had been, as he found himself with Blake's lips on his. The world around him disappeared, and once Harrison had recovered from the shock of what was happening, he put his arms around Blake and pulled him in closer, losing himself in that first kiss that he had wanted to happen for so many months.

After what could have been a few seconds or a century, Blake pulled his head away and looked into Harrison's eyes, speaking softly. "I know Nathan. If he's having some sort of row with his wife, then I feel like I need to say this, because I also know *you*. Don't you *ever* think you're not good enough for me. You are ten times the man he could ever be and don't you dare ever forget that. Because, do you know what Harrison Baxter? I love you. And we can wait around forever for each other to come to terms with that or we can just hold hands and get ready for the ride of our lives. So, which is it going to be?"

Harrison's heart was hammering in his chest. All he could do was nod breathlessly.

As it happened, words were not necessary. The

two of them kissed again, more fervently this time, as if they were trying to prove their intentions in the only way they knew how. The months of longing and curiosity melted away around them as they landed on the bed, grasping at areas of each other that they had been inaccessible for too long. The time for them to be together had finally arrived and, as Harrison was about to discover, nothing, not their reservations, not a smirking ex-boyfriend, not even a murder, was going to prevent Blake from making sure that every moment of it counted.

CHAPTER
TWELVE

The next morning, Blake opened his eyes and looked down at the sleeping blonde man whose head was resting on his chest. Even if this week away had gone absolutely nothing like the way either of them thought or hoped it would, they could at least take this away. Blake had realised that he needed to step up and be as sharp and insightful and brave as Harrison so clearly thought he was when he had gotten out of Sally's car and seen Nathan talking to him, with that same cocky and arrogant expression on his face. Faced with the two men who Blake had ever considered on the same level in his life, he had realised that he wanted to see only one of them happy, in fact only one of them meant anything to Blake whatsoever – and it certainly was not the one who had broken his heart.

Harrison stirred and slowly lifted his head with a yawn.

"Morning," Blake said, stroking his hair.

Harrison sat up and snuggled up to Blake. Even the touch of their bare shoulders against each other felt right. "What time is it?" Harrison asked, groggily.

"Does it matter?" Blake asked him.

Harrison leant forwards and kissed him. Even after they had been doing exactly that, and more, for most of the night, the jolt of excitement that coursed through Blake's body whenever their lips met had not faltered from its initial high point since the first one. "No," Harrison said. "I don't suppose it does. Though, you *have* still got a case to solve."

"That doesn't matter," Blake said. "You're far more important."

"Come on," Harrison said, kissing him briefly. "You've got nothing to prove now. We're an item, we're a thing. It's okay. So, come on." He kissed Blake again, then stood up and walked across to the kettle that was on the cabinet by the bed. It was already full of water, so Harrison flicked the switch and retrieved two cups from a nearby tray, before placing two teabags inside it. The sight of Harrison's body made Blake sigh with lust, but Harrison merely grinned at him and sat on the other side of the bed. "Come on then, Detective. If you were in charge of this case, what would be your next move?"

Blake sat up and folded his arms. "I'd go through all the facts that I knew so far with the rest of my officers."

Harrison leant across the bed and looked up at him. "In that case, reporting for duty, Sir."

Blake laughed. The mansion could be under siege by multiple killers and it would not have affected how happy he felt at that moment. "Okay," he said. "What do we know so far? Duncan Urquhart, the oldest brother of two who live in this mansion is murdered. We were witness to a hooded figure somehow walking across the lake where Duncan was fishing, and stabbing him to death."

"Except," Harrison pointed out, "that the forensics have said that can't have been exactly what happened because Duncan was already dead when the murder we thought we saw had happened." The kettle clicked, so Harrison stood up and poured the water into the cups.

"All the same though," Blake continued. "We ran out of the hut, and it was definitely Duncan lying in that lake. Rupert jumped in and pulled him to the bank. The police turn up and he's officially confirmed dead."

"Do you take sugar?" Harrison asked him.

"No thanks," Blake replied, staring into the

distance, playing back what he had seen that night in his head as Harrison brought the steaming cups across and climbed back into bed beside him.

"Who have we got as a suspect?" Harrison asked him, sipping from his cup.

"*Suspects*. Get you." Blake grinned.

Harrison laughed, then looked thoughtful. "You know when we were first walking towards the hut, down the path and towards the lakes for that dinner?"

Blake nodded.

"I didn't see Duncan in the boat in the lake, did you? I mean, I wasn't really looking for him, obviously, but would we have seen him?"

Blake considered this. "We were somewhat distracted, if you remember," he said. "We were talking, then Nathan turned up and was his usual *pain in the butt* self."

"What I'm trying to say," Harrison continued, "is that if Duncan had somehow already been murdered, then anyone could have done it, couldn't they? I mean, it could have been anybody underneath that hood."

"I suppose so, but-" Blake began, but then stopped. A thought had just landed in his head, one that he could not believe he had not already considered. "You're absolutely right," he said, stunned. "*Anybody* could have been underneath that hood! The two people who claim to have seen this hooded man, Rupert and Polly. Both of them claim that the figure was vandalising the property, smashing windows. That's not murderous behaviour."

"And a few chickens, don't forget," Harrison pointed out.

"You could get a dog or something to do that," Blake replied. "You wouldn't need to actually do it yourself." He thought for a few seconds to check that his theory made sense. "Rupert and Polly are the only ones to have seen this figure, Duncan always thought they were talking rubbish, none of the other guests have come forward saying they'd seen it and the only other possible witness, Patricia Urquhart is in a top room of the mansion, stuck in a wheelchair. What if, assuming that they're telling the truth, what if the hooded figure that was harassing them is a different hooded figure to the one that appeared to murder Duncan?"

Harrison frowned. "What do you mean?"

"Think about it. Polly's family, the Lomaxs, hate the Urquharts. I can easily picture them coming over here to try and damage the property, especially as this whole area of land used to belong to their family because of that old steam railway. Nothing better than a hood to hide your identity, so what if whoever murdered Duncan, was just using the hooded figure idea to hide their own crime?"

Harrison sipped his tea and nodded. "That makes sense. It still doesn't explain who it was though, or how they managed to pull off that whole walking across water thing or the fact that Duncan was already dead. I mean, we both saw him standing up, he looked alive enough to me when he was waving his arms about shouting."

Blake widened his eyes. "How do we know he was shouting? Did you hear anything?"

"Well, no. He was too far away."

Blake scratched the back of his head, thinking hard. Slowly, bit by bit, things were coming together. "*Exactly*. We were too far away to hear him shouting, we just saw him waving his arms about. It's possible that - No. Is it? *How?*"

"What?" Harrison asked, watching Blake talk to himself.

Blake turned to him, still wondering if what he was thinking was too ridiculous to be practical. "What if who we saw being '*murdered*' wasn't Duncan?"

Harrison stared at him in confusion, but before he could say anything else the sound of angry shouting began emanating from the corridor.

The two of them looked at each other, then quickly got dressed. As they hurried out of the room to see what was happening, Blake's mind was racing. He felt like he was close to putting everything together, but there were some vital pieces of the puzzle missing. All he needed to know was who exactly had lied to him since he had arrived at The Manor of the Lakes.

Once they were out on the corridor, they quickly realised that the shouting was coming from the reception area downstairs.

"...absolutely *preposterous!*"

"What do you think you're *doing*, Inspector?"

Blake rolled his eyes as they reached the top of the stairs and saw what was going on.

The reception area was in chaos. Gresham had Rupert in handcuffs and seemed to be attempting to frogmarch him out of the front door, made trickier by the fact that Polly was standing in the way and yelling at him. Blake strolled down the stairs and cleared his throat.

"Can I be of any assistance?"

Gresham glared at him. "Oh, why am I not surprised to see *you* here? No, thank you, Harte. The situation is perfectly under control, thank you, without you sticking your nose into it."

"This is absolutely absurd!" Rupert shouted. "What possible evidence have you got that I murdered my brother? I could *never* do that! I have a room full of witnesses that say I was the one who pulled him from the lake!"

"Yes, and I also have a forensic team telling me that your brother was long dead by the time you pulled him out, even before the apparent murder. I don't know how you did it, but I've got more than enough evidence that points the finger at you to keep a jury happy. Your brother made your life hell, didn't he?"

"Not to the extent where I could kill him!"

"You can tell me all about it at the station," Gresham replied, smiling broadly. "Come on! *Out*!"

As he finally managed to get his captive over the threshold, Rupert cried out to his wife who was now standing by the door, with her hands over her mouth, tears in her eyes. "*Polly*! Call our lawyer! I want every bit of legal representation we can afford!"

Polly watched her husband being taken off and as his voice faded away, she shut the door and put her head against it.

"Are you alright, Polly?" Blake asked her, putting a hand on her arm. "Stupid question, I know."

"Not really, no," Polly replied, before taking a long deep breath. "I am exhausted. I spent all night up at the hospital with Patricia, I don't know whether you heard, she had a seizure. It's a symptom of the lymphoma."

"I did hear, yes," Blake said gently. "Harrison said that Rupert stayed here?"

"Yes, that bloody inspector wanted to talk to him, not that it should have prevented him from going, but what can you do? Things aren't exactly normal round here at the moment."

"How is Patricia?"

"She's been discharged," Polly replied, turning round to face him at last. Blake was slightly taken aback by how exhausted Polly actually looked. She had bags underneath her eyes and her hair looked unkempt and dishevelled. "She's in the bar. If you'll excuse me, I think I need a long, hot bath."

Blake stepped aside to let her pass, then glanced at the bar, debating whether Patricia would be in any state to answer questions.

"What do you think?" Harrison asked him quietly once she was out of earshot. "Do you think Rupert did it?"

"He might have done," Blake replied. "But if he did, I doubt Gresham knows for sure. Do you fancy a drink?"

Patricia was sat at a table in the empty bar on her own, cradling a glass of water. As Blake and Harrison walked in, she looked up and watched them as they approached.

"You're still here?" she asked weakly.

"Yes," Blake replied, sitting down. "We thought we might be of some help."

Patricia took a sip of water, her hands trembling slightly. "One of my sons is dead, the other has just been arrested for his murder. I would try upping your game."

Blake nodded. It was difficult logic for him to argue with. "I understand you had to go to hospital last night?"

"Yes, I had a seizure. Not that the doctors seemed all that bothered. You'd think the state of the NHS at the minute, they'd want as many good reports as they can get, but I wasn't treated very well at all last night. A seizure and they *discharged* me! They always used to be so thorough. Nothing's like it used to be anymore." She sighed and stared out of the window, taking another sip of her water.

"You've had a lot of bad luck with your health, I understand?" Blake asked her. "Sorry, I don't mean to be personal."

"You policeman are just full of questions, aren't you?" Patricia replied, turning her wheelchair around while letting out a singular violent cough. "But yes. The big 'C' has rather haunted me throughout my life. It's most people's worst nightmare for it to even come up once. It's been a feature of my family for generations though. My mother died from it, hers was in the skin. Some of us are just dealt with an unfair lot in life, I suppose."

Again, she coughed loudly and violently, then began rubbing her chest, wincing.

"I get these chest pains," she murmured, closing her eyes. "Another symptom." Again, she began coughing, loudly and violently.

"Would you like another glass of water?" Harrison asked her, leaning forwards concerned.

"Yes, please," she answered in her raspy voice. "Try and make it as cold as you can, dear. It sooths my throat."

Harrison nodded and hurried to the bar with her

glass. Blake stood up and pulled his ecig out of his pocket. "You should put in a complaint about your treatment at that hospital, Patricia. The local one was it?"

"Yes," Patricia said as Harrison returned with the glass. "Mind you, the speed in which they were driving that ambulance, you wouldn't know it."

Blake nodded and smiled courteously. "Well, we just thought we'd check on you. Take care, Mrs Urquhart."

Blake strode out to the reception area, with his phone in his hand. He typed a message to Sally and pressed send, just as Harrison caught up with him.

"That poor woman," Harrison said quietly. "I've never known somebody so ill. How do you cope with something like that?"

"She's very ill, yes," Blake replied, distracted. "Harrison, when we were in her room when we first met her, do you remember what fell out of her toiletry bag?"

Harrison stared at him. "Her toiletry bag?"

"Remember when you knocked it over and the contents all spilled out?"

Harrison bit his lip thoughtfully. "Not really. Toothbrush, toothpaste, razor. The sort of thing you'd expect to find in a woman's toiletry bag."

"Exactly," Blake replied, striding up the stairs.

"Blake?" Harrison called, chasing after him. "What are you talking about? Where are you going?"

Blake stopped and waited for Harrison to catch up. "I know who killed Duncan. I can't believe I didn't realise it sooner. It's been there, staring at me the entire time, but with everything else, people walking across lakes, dead people being murdered, it clouded my thinking, which in fairness was exactly what it was supposed to do."

"You do? How?"

"I'll explain later. But I need you to get up to her room, and grab me that toiletry bag."

CHAPTER
THIRTEEN

resham slammed his car door and glared at Blake as he stormed towards him. "You've got some nerve calling me at this hour, Harte. Especially when I've got a suspect in custody."

"You won't regret it," Blake told him. "I promise. Just make your way to the hut, would you?"

Gresham frowned at him as Sally approached them, having arrived with him.

"You were right," she told him, shaking her head in disbelief. "We've got the footage should you need it."

"Thanks," Blake said to her. "Somehow I don't think we will be doing though. Shall we go?"

They all made their way down the car park and towards the lakes. The lights from the manor were the only thing lighting the way now as night had well and truly drawn in.

"You're sure about this, I take it?" Sally asked him. Blake nodded. It had taken him the rest of the day to gather everything and everyone he needed, but only after he had gone over and over the facts in his head, and it all tallied. While there were certain strands of information that were still unclear, he was hoping what was going to happen next would rectify that.

Blake pulled his mobile out of his pocket when they got to the hut and checked his screen. Harrison had text him, confirming that he was ready for Blake's signal.

Inside the hut, there were only two people missing from the group that Blake had gathered. Nathan looked up at Blake as he walked inside and held his hands out in a sign of confusion.

"Blake, what the hell's going on here?"

Blake merely smiled cheerfully at him. "All in good time, Nathan. Don't you worry about a thing."

The hut was arranged in exactly the same way it had been on the night of the murder. Blake had made absolutely sure that the table and chairs were all in the exact positions they had been when they had all been gathered in the hut. Davina was sat next to Nathan, her hands clasped together, staring at the wall. She looked extremely nervous.

"So can we get started, Harte?" Gresham asked, dramatically folding his arms together. "I am a *very* busy man, I don't have time to play your little games."

"Very nearly," Blake replied. "We're just waiting for – *Ah*, here they are now."

The door to the hut opened again and Patricia was wheeled in through the doorway. It was a tight fit, but with a slight effort, Polly managed to maneuverer the bulky wheelchair in.

"What on earth is all this about?" Patricia wheezed as Polly parked her by the table.

"Yes," Polly said, frowning at Blake. "I'd quite like to know that myself."

Blake placed his hands in his pocket and wandered across to the mini bar in the corner. "Thanks for coming everybody. I'm sorry to make this all so clichéd, but in this instance, I'm afraid it was necessary."

"Mr Harte, I am not a well woman," Patricia croaked, rubbing her chest, her bald head shining from the light hanging down from the ceiling. "I should be in bed."

"No, I know you're not well, Patricia." Blake said, leaning against the bar. "Still, I'm quite prepared to pause if you're chilly. You can always run back to your room and grab yourself a jumper?"

"Jesus Christ, Blake!" Nathan exclaimed, staring at Blake in disbelief. "That's low, even for you. Is it not enough you've made her come out here?"

Blake leant his head to the side and glanced at Patricia. "You want to explain, or shall I?"

Patricia stared at him. "I have absolutely no idea what you're talking about."

"Or maybe you, Polly?" Blake asked. "Or you, Davina?"

"Harte, what the hell are you blabbering on about?" Gresham snapped.

Blake nodded. "Fair enough, let's cut out the pretending. Starting with you, Patricia. The floor is yours. Tell the group. Explain to everybody - what it's like to have Munchausen's syndrome?"

Patricia stayed silent. She merely gazed back at Blake with a calm expression on her face.

Nathan scowled at Blake, clearly bemused. "Come again? *Munch-what* syndrome?"

"Munchausen's," Blake repeated. "It's a psychological disorder, where you pretend to be ill. There's plenty of reading about it online. People with Munchausen's tend to crave the attention that being gravely ill warrants."

"Harte, you should be absolutely *ashamed* of yourself!" shouted Gresham, standing up and looking outraged. "I saw this woman go into a seizure myself, how dare you accuse her of-"

"Yes, you did, didn't you? From what I understand, it was right in the middle of you interviewing her? Because Patricia craves attention, don't you? More than crave, it's an addiction," Blake continued. "And you know exactly what you need to do in order to get as much of it as possible, don't you?"

Patricia chuckled and stared at Blake with an expression of derision. "You think you're so clever, don't you? And may I ask, what proof you have of these wild and unfounded accusations?"

Blake nodded and produced the toiletry bag that Harrison had gotten him and placed it on top of the bar. Patricia's cold expression briefly faltered. "I would never have seen it, Patricia. Honestly, I was completely fooled. Everything you're doing – I mean, seriously. You're very, *very* good. The problem was that Harrison knocked over your toiletry bag when we came up to your room to tell you about Duncan's death." He unzipped the bag and rooted around it. "And when all the contents spilled out onto the floor, I didn't even realise I'd seen it. It's such a normal thing for a lady to have. Well, that is, it's normal for a lady who isn't going through the amount of chemotherapy you claim you are."

The whole room was now silent as Blake pulled out the razor that had clattered across the floor that night and had since been bothering him without Blake even realising it. He held it up for everybody to see. "There's even hairs just shy of the blades, Patricia. Repeated chemo, you lose it all. There should be nothing for you to shave. So why on earth would you need a shaving razor? Other than to keep up appearances. Oh, and let's not forget that violent cough that seems to have suddenly vanished since we started this discussion. I could *not* put my finger on what it was about you that was bothering me after our first encounter, then I realised. But me and Harrison were rather set up by someone pretending to be ill before we left here who actually had a remarkably similar fake cough to you. The difference being, of course, is that they didn't have your acting experience and there was nothing selfless in what you were doing. It was all just for you."

Everyone in the room turned to look at Patricia. She seemed completely unbothered by Blake's accusations, in fact Blake could tell she was rather enjoying herself.

"But why is all this relevant?" Blake continued. "You want to pretend to be incredibly ill, that's the syndrome. That's your life. I mean, it's a waste of hospital beds whenever you get that feeling you need attention and decide to fake a seizure or something but what does that have to do with the murder of Duncan Urquhart? Shall I go on, Patricia? I mean it *was* you, wasn't it? You did murder your son. You stabbed him to death, am I right? Because, let's make things perfectly clear here; if there's absolutely nothing wrong with you except a serious psychological condition, then there's absolutely no need for you to be sat in that wheelchair, is there? And you're just as capable of stabbing a man to death as the poor man currently in Inspector Gresham's custody?"

Sally cleared her throat and produced her mobile phone. "I went to the hospital you were at last night, Mrs Urquhart."

Patricia glared furiously at her. "I know my rights – you're not allowed access to my medical records without my consent!"

"Correct," Sally said, flicking through her phone. "But all I was really looking for was proof that you were there. That we *are* allowed to do. And a quick search for the CCTV cameras shows you climbing in and out of your bed, with no assistance whatsoever. You even at one point, take a wander down the corridor to, what I can only assume is complain at the receptionist?"

Sally held up her mobile for them all to see. The footage showed Patricia, waving her arms angrily at the receptionist, but standing up and walking around quite quickly as she did so.

"Good God," Nathan murmured.

Patricia looked down at the floor and sighed, then as calmly as ever, looked up at Blake. "You don't have any idea what it's like to be me, do you Detective? If you'd had the childhood I'd had – the beatings, the trauma, the abuse, then maybe you'd understand. When the only love and attention you get as a child is from the doctors and nurses caring for you when you've been beaten black and blue, is it any wonder you start to crave it? My parents didn't care for me. I was an accident, they told me that as many times as most children hear their mothers say '*I love you.*'"

"Why did you kill your son?"

Patricia ran her hand over her shaved scalp. "Because he didn't know. Duncan was not aware of my condition. As far as he was concerned, I was dying. But, instead of doing what any good son should do, caring for his sick mother, making sure I was comfortable, he was far more interested in making sure that my will was organised. My husband, God rest his soul, left all of this to me. And Duncan was after it. Anything to be able to lord it over everybody he came into contact with. As I explained to you, Detective, my son was not a nice man."

"No, which brings us to everybody else," Blake continued. "You see, everything that has happened here, this whole crazy plan to get rid of Duncan whilst making sure that the murderer, the true killer, was never caught, it couldn't be done by just you, could it?"

A whimper from the table told Blake that everything he had said was right. He looked down at the person who had made the noise. She had gone from staring at the wall, avoiding eye contact with everybody, to a shaking wreck.

"Davina?" Nathan said, staring at her. "What's wrong?"

"It's over, Davina," Blake said. "You don't have to pretend anymore. I don't know why you did it, but I'm not wrong am I? You *were* involved?"

"Oh, what the hell are you on about, *now?* You after trying to get my wife locked up, Blake? Is that it? You couldn't handle us breaking up, so what is this? Some sort of messed up revenge?" spat Nathan at Blake, before turning back to his quivering wife. "Would you calm down? What are you going on like this for?"

"Think about it, Nathan," Blake said. "That night. When we were watching that hooded figure. The only person who wasn't in the hut with us."

"She went to ring the police, because she saw whoever it was running about, that's what you told us!" Nathan exclaimed, staring between the two of them.

"I tried to tell you," mumbled Davina. "I hated myself. But we needed the money, Nathan."

"I don't understand what you're saying," Nathan replied, looking as serious as Blake had ever seen him. "You're not involved in all of this. How could you be?"

"Nathan, you know how much debt we're in. There were only so many final demand letters I could handle coming through our letterbox. Your job doesn't pay enough, neither does mine. I had to do something." She turned and looked at him imploringly, clearly trying to make him understand. "Everything we've been through together, it would all have been for nothing. I had to try and help *us.*"

Nathan stared at her in confusion. "No, but I don't get it. What did you do? You didn't murder someone, *she* did that."

Davina put her head in her hands. "I pretty much killed him. I helped make it happen, I as good as put that knife into him myself."

"Davina, you don't have to say anything else," Polly said sharply. "Listen to what he's saying, he's got no proof you did anything."

"Oh, Polly, for God's *sake!*" Davina shouted, her eyes wide and frantic. "It's *over*! I can't have this on my conscious anymore, I just can't."

"And I haven't forgotten about you, Polly," Blake said, sighing. "Because you were the key to the whole thing, weren't you? Without you, none of this would have even been possible."

"What are you talking about, Blake?" Polly exclaimed, outraged. "I was in here, with you! You can't pin a crime on me when I was one of the witnesses!"

"Yeah," Blake said, nodding. "A role you played to absolute perfection. You kept yourself well out of the way, because if something went wrong, like you say, you were one of the witnesses. How could you possibly be involved? Because one of you had to be in here, otherwise the illusion couldn't have happened. And that's exactly what it was, an illusion. But your role was the most important of all. Why were you involved though? Patricia was like a spider in the centre of a huge web of lies. Why were you one of her flies?"

Patricia laughed bitterly. "Because I found out about her little affair. I walked in on her with her arms around my son, except it was the wrong son, wasn't it, Polly?"

Polly closed her eyes and put her hands to her mouth.

"Problem was I actually did walk in on her. Duncan didn't see me, but she certainly did. Everything she thought she knew about me was gone. We suddenly knew each other's secrets. I was not everything I was claiming and she was having an affair with her husband's brother."

Blake looked up at Polly in surprise. "You were having an affair with *Duncan*? I thought you hated him."

"I did!" snapped Polly, throwing her hands down. "I absolutely despised him. But he had as much say over everything that happens in this house as he thought he did. He had been leaching over me for months and I thought that if I gave him what he wanted, it might save us a bit of time, or that at the very least, he might lay off his abuse of Rupert for a bit."

"But then your family started turning up as the hooded figure and causing you even more problems, didn't they?" Blake continued. "Nothing you could do about it, they'd made their minds up that they were going to cause trouble and there wasn't anything you could say to stop them. But it gave you an idea, Patricia. A way you could get rid of your son and stop him from trying to own this manor and keep yourself way out of the suspects list. And because you'd caught Polly in the act, you could bribe her.

"But I don't think, despite how carefully the whole thing was choreographed, that any of you three thought that forensics would be able to determine that the stab wounds weren't new." Blake glanced at Davina, who shook her head in response. "Once it was established that Duncan was already dead, it meant that you'd created one more impossible event than you'd intended to. And whilst you might just be able to get away with the notion of this mysterious stalker walking on water, the fact that what we were watching was essentially a corpse standing there defending itself from its attacker just wasn't possible, so the whole thing started to fall apart. It was just a case of working out which of the two events was intentional. Like I said all along, the hooded man walking across the lake to Duncan and stabbing him to death was so self-indulgent in itself, it could only be that one."

Gresham cleared his throat. "And how did they do it? Come on, Harte. Stop with the suspense, you're clearly dying to tell us."

Blake pulled his mobile out of his pocket and dialled Harrison's number. "If everybody could just look out the window?"

Nathan, Gresham and Sally all turned to stare out of the window. The view from the window allowed them to see right across the lake, where the silhouette of Harrison stood, waving.

"That's Harrison, waving over there." Blake added. "In case, anybody was wondering. And yes, that really is Harrison. Now, Sally – would you mind closing the curtains to the window?"

Sally did as she was told. After pulling the curtains across, so that the view of Harrison was blocked, she returned to her seat. All the time, Blake did not move from behind the mini bar, he just looked at Polly inquisitively. "How long does it take, Polly? Roughly? I've not done it before, I'm sort of improvising here, you see."

Polly didn't answer. She remained as silent as Patricia, who was just sat placidly in the wheelchair, taking in everything that was being said and done as if she was watching a documentary on television.

"That should probably do it," Blake said, shrugging. He came out from behind the mini bar and put the phone back to his ear. "Are you ready, Harrison?"

"Yeah, just," Harrison answered, down the phone, sounding out of breath.

"Good," Blake said, pulling the curtain back across. They all stared out of the window. There was Harrison's silhouette, still waving.

"What are we supposed to be looking at?" Nathan snapped. "It's exactly the same view."

"You'd think so, wouldn't you?" Blake replied. "Ok, Harrison," he said into his phone. "Do your thing."

On Blake's instruction, Harrison could be seen walking towards the lake, but instead of stopping at the water's edge, just like the hooded figure had that night, Harrison began walking across the surface of the lake.

"This is really weird," Harrison said down the phone. "Even though I know what's happening,"

"Well?" Gresham exclaimed. "How is he doing that?"

"If everyone would just like to step outside," Blake answered, indicating the door. "I think everything should start to become a bit clearer."

Leading the way, Blake opened the door and led Gresham, Nathan and Sally outside, leaving the other three still sat in silence at the table. "Notice anything different?" Blake asked, once they were outside.

Gresham looked around him in confusion and stared at the lake in front of him. "Wait a minute," he gasped. "We've moved. This isn't where we came in, it's all different."

Blake looked across the lake to where Harrison was still standing on the surface of the water. "It's interesting to read some of the interviews with magicians. A lot of the best tricks rely on the fact that the way they're done is so opaque that the audience wouldn't even consider it as a solution, and it's exactly the same in this instance. What none of us ever thought to remember when we were staring out at the lake with Duncan's body floating in it was the fact that the hut is in the centre of two lakes. And what you're looking at now, is what we saw through the window on the night of the murder. We just didn't realise that we were looking at a completely different lake to the one we thought we were.

"I would never have worked it out. Not in a million years. Until I was in standing in Lionel Lomaxs workshop where he had a model railway of what this place used to look like when the steam trains were still in business. You see, Urquhart Manor is where the end of the line would have been. What was it Lionel said to us, Sally?"

Sally was looking left to right between the two lakes like she was watching a tennis match. "That the steam engines would turn round and take the passengers back up the other way?"

"Exactly," Blake said. "Now, if we were talking about electric trains, the sort of thing that can run backwards and forwards all day without any problems, then the whole theory is defunct. But for steam trains, it's different. It's not safe for them to go long distances backwards so they need something to make them turn round so that they can go back the other way." They all stared back at him, clueless. "A turntable," finished Blake. "And if a turntable is capable of spinning around an entire steam engine on its own, a wooden hut with a few people inside is nothing. And a turntable is exactly what was at the end of the line on Lionel Lomaxs model, so it had to be somewhere. The fact that the Urquharts had left that semaphore signal sticking up out the ground for posterity's sake meant that maybe there was something else, but this time, hidden from view. Right underneath the hut."

He indicated that they should follow him back into the hut. As he walked back inside, he indicated to Harrison that he should join them.

"But how was it operated?" Sally asked, looking dumbfounded.

"It's all under this mini bar," Blake replied, pushing it aside slightly so that they could all see. Secreted just underneath the minibar was a switch with buttons. "Press one button, and if you look out the window, we're turning. It's subtle, it's smooth, if you didn't know you were moving, which we didn't, you'd have no idea whatsoever."

They all gazed out the window as the lake slowly came around and into view again. A few moments later, the door opened again and Harrison walked in, trying not to look anybody in the eye, apart from Blake who gave him a small grin to congratulate him on a job well done.

"But how was he standing on the water?" Nathan asked, still looking as dazed and shell-shocked as he had since Davina's confession.

Blake glanced at Sally. "The steel panels from the workshop. I knew there was no feasible way for someone to do that without something to stand on, which is why it was the first thing I looked for that night. Of course, I was looking for my evidence in completely the wrong lake. Stick some poles in and you have a path to the centre of the lake where you'd set up the boat where '*Duncan*' was sat. It's still there, because since there's been police buzzing around all the time since the murder, you haven't had time to remove it. But why bother? After all, it's not in the lake where the murder happened. Not hard to get hold of them from your father's workshop, I'm presuming, Polly? When the rest of the Lomaxs were all out of the way."

Blake walked out from behind the mini bar and crossed his arms, watching Polly, Patricia, and Davina with a serious expression on his face. "So, now we know all that – it's a lot easier to piece together exactly what we saw that night. Patricia, when did you kill Duncan?"

"A couple of hours before hand," Patricia replied

airily, staring out of the window again, as if she was watching it all happen in front of her again. "I'd followed him into one of the bathrooms upstairs and done it then. Greed, that's all this is based on, Mr Harte. And my son was full of it. He wanted this entire manor left to him when I died. Ironically, if he hadn't had forced me to change my will, I probably would have left him most of it. The last thing he saw was his mother standing before him for the first time in years. That look of shock on his face when he realised what was happening – I expect that'll stay with me. Anyway, the body was dragged down here. Once you were all inside this hut, everything was set."

Blake turned to Polly, indicating that it was her time to talk now. At first, she seemed reluctant, but then she seemed to give up fighting and just sighed. "It's like you said, everything was carefully worked so that the timing was just right. Patricia played the hooded figure and then Davina played the Duncan you thought you were watching defend himself."

Davina looked at Nathan, regret and fear in her eyes. "Once I'd ran out of here when I said I'd call the police, I ran to where we'd got Duncan's body. Polly turned the hut round and I had to push the boat and his body out into the lake. Once everything was in place, I ran 'round to the other lake and got into position." She shook her head in disbelief. "It was all so carefully planned. Patricia went through Duncan's wardrobe after she'd killed him and got out a similar looking suit and cap to the one he was wearing, which was waiting in the second boat. All I had to do was put the suit and cap over what I was already wearing."

"And then you and Patricia just acted out the murder for us." Blake continued. "She was in the hood, pretended to stab you and once you'd fallen in the water, apparently dead, we all tried to get out to help Duncan. But Polly had locked the door. In the time it took you to run across the hut, and unlock the door, with some brilliant fumbled hands acting to buy you some more time, the hut had turned back round again to face the right way and the whole trick was complete. As far as we were concerned, we'd just seen the figure stab Duncan to death, his body was lying in the water and the hooded figure had completely disappeared. And while we were fussing around on this side, Rupert pulling his body out of the lake, me looking in the water for platforms, the truth was just behind us."

Stunned silence enveloped the entire hut. After a few moments, Nathan turned to Davina, disgust etched across his face. "How could you? I dropped *everything* for you. Everything I knew, everything I thought I was."

Blake tried to react as little as possible to what he was saying. He did not even feel in the slightest bit smug or pleased – if anything, he felt sorry for the man who had broken his heart. He had seen enough couples be ripped apart because of one or the other's crimes and it was not something he would wish on anybody.

"You've got to believe me, Nath," Davina pleaded, attempting to take hold of his hand. "I did it all for *us*. The money Polly was offering me to help out could have wiped away our debts and left us with some to spare, and to make an actual difference to our lives!"

Nathan wrenched his hand away from her and stood up, glaring down at her. "We'd have managed. You think we're the first couple to have money issues? But instead you chose to get yourself involved with this insanity. How did I ever think…?" His voice faded away as he glanced at Blake who could not maintain eye contact with him for more than a few seconds. Without another word, Nathan flung the door to the hut open and stormed out into the night. Blake watched him leave and sighed.

"Well. Inspector Gresham, Sally, I think you can probably deal with things from here?"

Gresham cleared his throat. "Yeah, yeah I expect we can, Harte, I fully expect we can. Sergeant Matthews, would you mind calling for some assistance? I think we've got a lot to discuss with the three ladies here."

Blake looked around the hut. Davina was sobbing silently into her arms, clearly at a loss at how her life had gone so drastically wrong. Polly dropped heavily into the chair recently vacated by Nathan, and

Patricia continued watching proceedings with a vague air of interest. It was as if she had fully accepted that this moment would eventually arrive and was just calmly waiting for the next step in proceedings.

As Gresham began arresting the three of them and Sally spoke into her radio for assistance, Harrison took a step forwards and put his arm on Blake's shoulder. "You can go after him you know. I understand."

"Why would I need to-"

"Because the reason I fell in love with you in the first place was because you're the most compassionate man I've ever met," Harrison said firmly. "There's things you want to say to him and you probably won't get another chance. Plus I can see you're upset. Go. It's fine. I'll go back to the room and start packing. I'm guessing we're not going to be staying here another night?"

Blake glanced around the hut again. "No, probably not."

Harrison smiled and, despite the situation, Blake felt a respect and adoration that he had not felt for a long time. "Come on then."

CHAPTER
FOURTEEN

As it was, Nathan had not gone far. As Blake and Harrison walked back towards the mansion together, Blake saw him sitting underneath a tree with his head in his hands a little further down the path.

Without a word, Harrison squeezed Blake's hand and kissed him on the cheek, then set off back to the mansion on his own. Blake smiled at him then took a deep breath before slowly walking up behind his ex-boyfriend.

Nathan had his back to him and did not even turn round, but as Blake got nearer he murmured,

"Do you still smoke?"

Blake pulled his ecig out of his pocket. "Not really. Now and again. I don't have any on me though, sorry."

For the first time, Nathan turned to look up at him, his eyes red and puffy. It was the first time Blake had ever seen him look anything close to emotional. All the bravado and arrogance seemed to have completely deserted him. "I bet you're loving this, aren't you?"

Blake took a long suck on his ecig and blew the vapour out thoughtfully, as he sat himself down besides Nathan. "No. Maybe I would have done once. There was a time I would have paid to see you anywhere near as heartbroken as you made me, but no. I feel sorry for you."

"You pity me, you mean."

"No, I feel sorry for you, that's all. It's a lot to come to terms with. You thought you knew her. But then again, I thought I knew you, so I guess it shows how much *that* matters in the long run."

Nathan didn't reply. Blake filled the silence with another long suck on his ecig. "Is your money situation really that bad?"

Nathan let out a short bitter laugh and nodded. "Yeah. I don't think it's anything that can't be sorted out if I speak to the right people in the banks. There's a solution to everything, right? That's what you always used to say."

Blake nodded. "Yeah. They'll be ways. A bit of hard graft and resilience, talk to your mum, she'll help you out. She always used to. Or, failing that, you're smart enough to work something out for yourself. That gift of the gab has got to be good for something, right?"

Nathan pulled Blake's ecig out of his hand and inhaled on it deeply. As he blew the vapour out, he stared out towards the lake where they had all been fooled, which was just visible through the hedges in front of them. "I take it you and your man are a thing now? I recognise that look in you. I saw it straight away when I first clapped eyes on you in reception the other day."

Blake glanced up at the mansion where Harrison was currently packing his bags to return to Harmschapel. "Yeah. Yeah we are."

Nathan took another hit on the ecig and passed it back to him. "He seems like a decent fella. A bit wet, but that's probably just me. I hope you're happy together."

Blake resisted the urge to roll his eyes. "He's the most decent, kind hearted, genuine guy I've ever met."

Nathan nodded, a slight undertone of hurt betraying the look of calmness he was clearly trying to convey. "Good. My life has gone down the toilet, so I guess karma really is a thing, right?"

This time, Blake was unable to prevent his eyes

from rolling. "That's so you. You're not the worst off in this situation, you do realise that?"

Nathan gazed at him bemused. "How do you work that out?"

Blake shook his head in disbelief. "Rupert? He's currently in custody in a police station for a crime he didn't commit. And when he gets out, it'll be to the realisation that his mother and wife are being jailed for murder. His brother is dead and God knows how long he'll be able to keep hold of this place. There are people worse off than yourself, you know."

Nathan shrugged. "It's not my life though, is it?"

As Blake looked at the man he had once been head over heels in love with, he was surprised by how little he felt for him. Even when they had come face to face with each other again after so long, a mere two days ago, Blake had been left feeling conflicted and confused by how he felt, but now he knew it could not be clearer. Nathan was right, there was a definite element of pity.

"I've got to ask you this, Nathan. I know the timing is crap, but if I don't ask you now, I don't think I'll ever get the chance again."

"Timing never was your strong point, Blakey. It was the one imperfection about you."

Blake paused, then finally said, "Why did you do that to me? I thought we were happy. I honestly thought you and me were going to spend the rest of our lives together. Get engaged, marry, maybe even start a family. Then I come home one night and find you in bed with her. Why?"

Nathan stared out towards the lake again. "I don't know, Blake. Maybe things weren't quite as perfect as you thought they were. I can't explain it, my feelings just changed."

"There's ways of dealing with that, Nathan. But you chose the coward's way out. Just like Davina did, you chose the way that would cause the most hurt to everyone else, rather than having difficult conversations. You just *did it.* And that's what hurt the most. But I guess I should thank you, really."

Nathan looked up at him as Blake stood up and put his ecig back in his pocket. "Thank me? Why?"

"Because you made me run away and have to start all over again," Blake replied. "And because of that, I met Harrison and the people that I work with now and I'm happier than I've ever been before. I just didn't realise quite how happy I was till this moment. So I guess now there's only one thing I need to say to you."

Again, the bravado in Nathan's face had disappeared. He looked sad and alone and scared of what was to come in his life, just like Blake had done all those months ago.

"And that's goodbye, Nathan." Blake finished. "Something I never got to say before. Goodbye. I genuinely hope you have a happy life."

They looked into each other's eyes for a few

moments, before the hut door opened and Patricia, Polly and Davina were led out by Sally and Gresham. Blake turned to look at his ex again, but Nathan was watching Davina being walked towards the blue flashing lights that had become visible in the distance. Without another word, Blake walked away, leaving Nathan standing silent and alone beneath the tall oak tree.

An hour later, Blake pulled his case up from the ground and dropped it into the boot of his car. Harrison leant against the car, watching Blake as he slammed the door shut.

"You alright?" he asked.

Blake turned to him and smiled, before wrapping his arms around his boyfriend. "Yeah. I'm more than alright. I'm fantastic."

He pulled Harrison closer and kissed him, savouring every second.

"I'd like to think I'm somewhat responsible for this," came a voice from behind them.

The two of them separated and Blake laughed. "And in what way would *that* be, Sally-Ann?"

Sally cringed at the use of her full name and slapped Blake on the arm. "Because my drunken, messy behaviour that night in the pub meant that the longing you two have for each other got stronger, culminating in this romantic climax?"

"Yeah, that's you," Blake replied, grinning. "All

heart." He pulled Sally in and hugged her tightly. "It's been so good to see you."

"And you," Sally said. "Let's do it again soon, more gin and less murder next time though. That being said, it was great working with you again. We make an unstoppable team."

"We've got one more addition now," Blake said, pulling Harrison in to join in with the hug. "An unstoppable trio, that's us."

"Welcome to the team, Harrison," Sally said, putting her arm around him. "Just remember though, you'll have to keep up with me and Blake's drinking habits when we three meet again."

"Having seen the way you are after just a few gins, I think I should be alright," Harrison replied, laughing.

Sally let out a cry of faux outrage, then pulled Harrison in tighter in revenge. "I'm honestly so happy for you both. Do me a favour and don't go sleeping with any women, Harrison. I can't deal with him being all depressed again. He's dead boring in that mind-set."

"Do you mind?" Blake exclaimed.

"I won't, I promise," Harrison replied, laughing again. He turned to Blake. "I'll wait in the car, you two say your goodbyes. Don't let it be too long before I get to drink you under the table though, Sally."

"Try and keep me away, sunshine," Sally told him, winking at him. As Harrison climbed into the car, Sally squeezed Blake's hand and smiled happily. "He's so much more confident now than when I first met him. You did that, you know. I'm proud of you."

"He always had it in him," Blake replied, shaking his head. "I'm just pleased he feels better about himself."

Sally nodded. "Hey, before you go. Guess what? Gresham is *fuming* you got to the bottom of all this before him. He's told me not to tell anyone at the station about any of this. So obviously, I rang the station after he'd gone and told gobby Mary on the front desk. The whole station will know within the hour."

Blake laughed loudly and gave her one last huge hug. "I love you."

"I love you too. Now, go. Your boyfriend awaits."

Blake nodded, then released his grip on his best friend and opened the driver's seat of the car. "See you soon."

He climbed into the car and closed the door, before turning to Harrison. "Ready?"

Harrison nodded. "Best holiday ever, right?"

Blake laughed as he started the car and the radio came on.

After doing up his seatbelt, Harrison turned up the volume on the radio. "I love this song!"

Blake watched him dancing cheerfully in his seat for a few moments, a happier and lighter man, the effects from the past year of his life seemingly melting away before his eyes, and smiled warmly at him. Then, he pulled down the window and waved to Sally as they set off down the path towards the main road. They had a long drive ahead of them, but with Harrison by his side, Blake would have driven for more hours than he cared to think about.

ONE WEEK
LATER

Harrison opened the door to The Dog's Tail pub and was surprised to see it as busy as he could ever remember. A large sign near the bar told him exactly why: '*HARMSCHAPEL KARAOKE NIGHT – HAVE YOU GOT THE TALENT?'* Wondering why Blake had asked him to come along to a night that Harrison knew Blake would rather avoid entirely, he pushed his way through the crowd and found the table that Blake's colleagues, Mini Patil, Billy Mattison, and Michael Gardiner were sitting at. Jacqueline was sitting next to Gardiner and looked delighted as Harrison approached them.

"*Harrison*!" Jacqueline exclaimed happily, passing him a pint. "So glad you could make it! Please have this on me. I feel like I owe you an apology after everything that happened on that awful holiday."

Harrison gratefully accepted the pint. "It's not your fault. How were you supposed to know?"

Jacqueline shook her head as she sipped from the large wine glass she had in front of her. "That Polly was always a cow at school. I never did like her. *Murder* though! Who'd have thought it?"

Harrison shrugged and took a large gulp of his pint before turning to the other officers from Harmschapel police station. "How are you?"

Mattison raised his own beer at Harrison in greeting. "Not bad thanks, Harrison! Good to see you mate."

"Where's Blake?"

Patil glanced at the others and grinned. "You'll see. There's a reason you've been invited here tonight."

Gardiner folded his arms and shook his head in his usual grumpy manner. "I don't know how you managed to talk me into getting involved in all this."

"Because you've been promised two pints and my own personal little surprise when we get home for your trouble," Jacqueline said sternly, though she tapped him playfully on the nose. It was not an action that Gardiner appeared to appreciate.

A moment later, a pair of arms wrapped themselves around Harrison. "Hello gorgeous man."

Harrison looked up at Blake and kissed him before asking him "What is all this about?"

Blake sighed and rolled his eyes. "You know when we were sat in the hotel and you told me that one of your aspirations was for a bloke to serenade you? Did you actually mean it?"

Harrison glanced at the others in embarrassment. "Well, it was just a silly thing-"

"Yes, but did you actually mean it?"

"I guess so, yeah."

Blake sighed, reserved. "Damn. Well, in that case, you better get comfortable."

He stood up straight and waved to Robin the barman, who nodded in response and passed Blake a microphone. "Come on then, you lot. You know what to do."

Harrison stared at the officers of Harmschapel as they all stood up and walked towards the centre of the pub, all of them with their back to him. Jacqueline too got up and joined them, squeezing a clueless Harrison on the arm as she passed. "You're going to just *love* this, darling!"

As the crowd of people made room for them to gather in the centre of the pub, Blake gave one last nod to Robin and a familiar song began to play over the loudspeaker. Harrison gasped. It was the song he had heard in the car as they had been leaving the mansion and as Blake raised the microphone he had been passed to his mouth, Harrison realised that he was indeed about to be serenaded.

"You're just too good to be true,
Can't take my eyes off of you
You'd be like heaven to touch
I wanna hold you so much,
At long last, love has arrived,
And I thank God I'm alive
You're just too good to be true
Can't take my eyes off of you,"

sang Blake, as the others began a clearly rehearsed dance behind him. Harrison was amazed that on top of Blake's other talents, he also had an excellent singing voice. By far the funniest sight was Gardiner who had a face of thunder as the familiar instrumentals of the song crashed in and he half-heartedly joined in with the routine the others were performing behind Blake to the cheers and laughter of everyone else in the pub. Harrison could not take the look of pure joy off his face as he watched them all dance as Blake continued singing, directing every word of the song to Harrison. Then, for the final chorus, Mattison ran up to him and pulled him with the rest of them. Blake put his arm around him and, completely unbothered by everyone watching, they all belted out the lyrics. As the song came to a close, the roof was practically lifted by the sound of the cheering and whooping around them.

As he kissed his boyfriend again, Harrison's mind, for the first time since this incredible man had landed in his life, was free of doubt, anxiety, and self-deprecation. Although everything he had known had been thrown up in the air and landed around him in varying degrees of disarray, it all felt right, and that was all Harrison had ever wanted.

"Looks like we're a hit," Blake said to him. "There's just one thing we need to sort so that everybody is happy for us."

Harrison frowned. "What's that?"

Blake raised a disdainful eyebrow. "That bloody goat."

Blake Harte will be back soon for a fourth mystery soon!

Keep up to date with Robert Innes' new releases at:
facebook.com/RobertInnesAuthor

Made in the USA
Columbia, SC
01 May 2019